The Necromancer

&

the Golden Knight

ALIX ALORA

Published by CNG Studios LLC

For permission requests, please contact the publisher at the address below:

CNG Studios LLC

Phone: (786) 512-9978 • E-mail: info@cngstudios.com

ISBN: 978-1-965953-11-2

This is a work of fiction. Names, characters, businesses, places, events, and incidents are either the product of the author's imagination or used in a fictitious manner. Any resemblance to actual persons, living or dead, or actual events is purely coincidental.

Cover design by CNG Studios LLC

Author's site: www.alixalora.com

First Edition

Printed in the United States of America

ALSO BY ALIX ALORA

The Soul-Tether Saga

The Necromancer & the Golden Knight
The King of Hollows (Coming Soon)

For those who speak to the dead, because the living wouldn't listen.

Acknowledgements

To those who have stood beside me through every wild idea, every impossible dream, and every moment when the path forward seemed unclear—thank you for your patience, your unwavering support, and your absolute refusal to let me give up on myself. You believed in the stories I needed to tell before I found the courage to tell them.

To my eternal partner, my soul-tether in this world—you are the proof that love is both the anchor that keeps me grounded and the wings that help me fly. Every word in this book is a testament to what we've built together. Thank you for choosing me, every single day.

And to my children, my fierce and wonderful heroes—you teach me daily what it means to be brave, to question the world, to fight for what matters. Your belief in me has carried me through the darkest drafts and the longest nights. This book exists because you showed me that magic is real; it lives in the way you see the world. May you always know your own strength, and may you always choose love over fear.

You are my why. You are my everything. This story is yours as much as it is mine.

With gratitude and a touch of neon-pink magic,

Alix Alora

Chapter One

THE MIDNIGHT TAX

The silver spade bit into the soil with a satisfying thud.

Elara Vance didn't mind the manual labor; it was good for the glutes, and the dead were generally better conversationalists than the living. At least the dead didn't complain about the price of eggs or the scandalous length of her hemlines.

The Oakhaven Cemetery had a particular quality to its darkness that Elara had always appreciated. It wasn't the oppressive, suffocating black of a cellar or a cave. It was the soft, velvety darkness of a world that had simply turned off the lights and decided to rest. The ancient yew trees that lined the graveyard walls filtered the moonlight into silver-green patterns that danced across the weathered headstones, and somewhere in the distance, an owl called out its hunting song.

Perfect working conditions.

"Honestly, Arthur," Elara said, wiping a smudge of dirt from her nose with a lace-trimmed sleeve that had seen far better nights. "If you didn't want to tell me where the family jewels were buried, you should have written a clearer will. Now look at us. It's midnight, I'm sweating through my second-best corset, and you're just a floating head with a bad attitude."

The ghost of Sir Arthur hovered over his own tombstone with the indignant posture of a man who had spent his living years perfecting the art of being affronted. His translucent mustache twitched with barely contained outrage, and his spectral form flickered between visibility and invisibility as his emotions surged.

"It is the principle of the thing, girl!" Arthur's voice had the peculiar quality of all ghost-speech—it didn't come from any particular direction, but seemed to emanate from the air itself, settling directly into Elara's consciousness. "Necromancy is a foul art! My bones deserve the sanctity of the earth, not to be pawned off to settle my fool grandson's gambling debts!"

"It's recycling, Arthur. Get over yourself," Elara grunted, tossing a shovelful of dirt over her shoulder with practiced efficiency. The hole was nearly deep enough now—another foot and she'd reach the casket. "Besides, your great-grandson is about to lose the family estate to a very unpleasant man with very expensive tastes in violence. I'm basically a high-stakes accountant with a shovel. You should be thanking me."

"I should be resting in peace!"

"You've been dead for two hundred years, Arthur. If you haven't found peace by now, that's a you problem."

She stopped digging and raised her hands, flexing her fingers in the moonlight. The air around her fingernails began to glow with a soft, neon-pink necrosis—her signature color, the thing that had marked her as different from the moment her powers manifested. Most necromancers dealt in sickly greens or bone-whites, their magic the color of decay and rot. But Elara's magic had always been... vibrant. It was the color of a sunset that had stayed up too late and had a few drinks. The color of peonies and passion and defiance.

It was the color that had gotten her arrested seventeen times in the past three years.

She was about to make it eighteen.

But before she could snap the spirit back into its skeletal remains—a simple enough procedure that would have let Arthur's ghost communicate with his idiot descendant and reveal the location of the hidden jewels—the temperature in the graveyard dropped twenty degrees.

And it wasn't the "chilly ghost" kind of cold. It was the "burning, righteous judgment" kind of cold—the kind that smelled of ozone and expensive incense and the particular brand of self-righteousness that only came from a man who had never missed a morning prayer or questioned a single order in his entire life.

Elara's magic flickered and died. She knew that cold. She'd felt it seventeen times before.

A shadow fell over the grave, blocking out the moonlight. It wasn't a ghostly shadow—those were wispy, translucent things that barely registered against the dark. This shadow was heavy. Solid. It had weight and presence and the unmistakable clink of fifty pounds of blessed armor moving with military precision.

"Elara Vance," a voice boomed—deep, resonant, and unfortunately very attractive in that "forbidden paladin" sort of way that really should not have made her stomach do a small, traitorous flip. "By the authority of the High Order and the Decree of the Living, you are under arrest for Unauthorized Spectral Reanimation."

Elara didn't even look up. She didn't need to. She would recognize that voice anywhere—it had featured prominently in several very inappropriate dreams and at least three elaborate revenge fantasies.

Sir Kaelen. The "Golden Lion" of the Paladin Order. The man who probably polished his moral compass every morning right after he polished his breastplate and his insufferable sense of duty.

"Kaelen, darling," she sighed, finally leaning on her spade and looking up with an expression of profound weariness. "You're five minutes early. I'm impressed. Usually, you time these dramatic entrances for maximum inconvenience. Have you been taking classes?"

He was standing on the edge of the pit she'd dug, looking like a literal god of justice who had decided to moonlight as a professional killjoy. His golden plate armor shimmered even in the dim moonlight, each piece perfectly maintained, not a scratch or dent visible despite the fact that she knew he'd been fighting Void-creatures at the northern border just three days ago. The hilt of his broadsword glowed with a faint, annoying white light—the Order's trademark "Holy Light" that seemed designed specifically to give necromancers like her a headache.

His helmet was tucked under one arm, revealing a face that could have been carved by a particularly talented and sexually frustrated sculptor. Sharp jawline, high cheekbones, eyes the color of a mid-day sky, and an expression of perpetual, simmering irritation that somehow only made him more attractive.

Elara hated him. Mostly because she didn't actually hate him, and that was far more inconvenient.

"I haven't even gotten to the 'evil' part yet," Elara protested, gesturing at the partially excavated grave with her muddy spade. "This is just preparatory excavation. I'm practically an archaeologist. Very scholarly. Very respectable."

"You're elbow-deep in the grave of a Duke, Elara." Kaelen's voice was tired—bone-tired in a way that made something in Elara's chest twist uncomfortably. "There is a signed warrant for your detention. Again. The seventeenth warrant, to be precise. The magistrate is running out of parchment."

"It's an organized grave, Kaelen," she countered, gesturing to the neat piles of dirt she'd arranged by soil composition. "And you have a smudge on your breastplate. Right there, over your heart. It's very distracting. Do you want me to polish it with a ghost? Arthur is bored anyway and has strong opinions about proper armor maintenance."

She could see the exact moment Kaelen's jaw tightened—a small muscle jumping beneath his skin as he fought the urge to either laugh or throttle her. She'd become expert at identifying that particular expression over the years.

"Hand over the spade, Elara," he said, stepping closer. His heavy boots crunched on the gravel path between graves, each step deliberate and controlled. "Before I have to carry you back to the dungeon. I have had a very long day, I haven't slept in forty-eight hours, and I am in no mood for your... whatever this is."

He paused, and something flickered across his face—exhaustion, yes, but also something older. A shadow that had nothing to do with the moonlight. "Berenger would have just knocked you unconscious and dragged you back by your ankles. He always said I was too soft on heretics. Said it would get me killed someday."

The words came out flat, automatic, like he was reciting someone else's script. But Elara caught the way his jaw tightened when he said the name, the way his hand flexed on his sword hilt as if the mention of his old mentor made him want to reach for something solid.

"Berenger sounds delightful," Elara said. "Does he polish his personality along with his armor, or does that just come naturally?"

"He taught me everything I know about being a paladin," Kaelen said, and there was something in his voice that Elara couldn't quite parse. Pride? Resentment? Both? "Everything about duty, sacrifice, putting the mission above..." He stopped himself, shook his head. "The spade, Elara."

She handed it over, but she filed that moment away. The way Kaelen's voice had caught. The way he'd stopped himself from finishing that sentence.

Everything about putting the mission above what, exactly?

Whatever this is. As if he didn't know exactly what this was. As if they hadn't been performing this particular dance for three years now—her pushing boundaries, him enforcing them, both of them pretending they didn't feel the crackle of something dangerous and electric in the space between.

Elara climbed out of the grave with a feline grace that belied the mud caked on her boots and the exhaustion pulling at her bones. She'd been working since sunset, and her back ached from the digging, but she'd be damned if she'd let him see weakness.

She stopped just inches from him, well within the "danger zone" of his personal space, close enough to smell the ozone-and-leather scent that clung to his armor, close enough to see the golden flecks in his blue eyes catch the moonlight.

"You know," she said conversationally, "seventeen arrests in three years is really quite impressive. Almost as if you're specifically assigned to watch me."

"You're the only active necromancer in Oakhaven," Kaelen replied, his voice carefully neutral even as she felt the heat radiating off him—that peculiar warmth that all paladins carried, like they'd swallowed a piece of the sun. "It's not personal."

"Everything's personal, darling."

"Don't call me that."

"What should I call you? 'Sir' feels too formal for someone I've shared seventeen dungeon stays with. 'Kaelen' feels too familiar. Maybe I should just call you—"

"Elara." Her name was a warning. A plea. Both.

She smiled—bright and sharp and utterly unrepentant. "There we go. See? We're making progress."

Arthur's ghost materialized between them with the timing of a particularly dramatic theater critic. "Are we going to stand here flirting all night, or is someone going to arrest someone? I have a schedule."

"We're not flirting," Kaelen and Elara said in perfect unison, which rather undermined the point.

Arthur's translucent eyebrow rose in a way that suggested two hundred years of death hadn't dulled his capacity for skepticism. "Of course not. My mistake. Carry on with your very professional and not-at-all charged arrest, Sir Paladin."

Kaelen's hand closed around Elara's elbow—gentle but firm, the touch of a man who'd spent years learning exactly how much force was needed to subdue without harming. "Come on. The High Priest is waiting."

That killed the levity faster than a knife to the throat.

"Valerius wants to see me?" Elara's voice came out sharper than she'd intended. "This isn't just another night in the cell?"

Through his grip on her arm, she felt Kaelen's pulse spike—a flutter of something that felt suspiciously like anxiety. "No. This is… different."

"Different how?"

"Let's just say the magistrate is tired of filling out paperwork for your releases. They've found a more permanent solution."

Elara's stomach dropped. "Execution?"

"No." Kaelen's eyes met hers, and in their depths, she saw something that looked almost like an apology. "Worse."

Kaelen didn't answer. He led her toward the cemetery gates, where two more paladins waited with torches and suspicious expressions. As they passed through the wrought-iron archway, Elara cast one last glance back at Arthur's grave—still half-excavated, the ghost hovering over it with an expression caught between relief and disappointment.

"This conversation isn't over, Arthur!" she called back.

"Oh, I'm quite certain it isn't," the ghost muttered. "Nothing with you is ever over. It just gets more complicated."

The cemetery gates clanged shut behind them, and Elara allowed herself to be escorted toward the looming spires of the Cathedral, her mind racing through every possible reason the High Priest himself would want to see her.

None of them were good.

But at least Kaelen was beside her. Whatever was coming, she wouldn't face it alone.

Even if "together" currently meant "handcuffed to my nemesis."

Chapter Two

THE DUNGEON DEBRIEF

The dungeons of the High Order did not, in fact, have excellent lighting for Elara's skin tone.

She'd checked three different corners of her cell, testing the way the flickering mage-lights hit her face, and the verdict was unanimous: the sickly yellow hue was a catastrophe. They cast a jaundiced pallor that made her look less like a powerful necromancer and more like a three-day-old head of lettuce someone had forgotten at the back of a market stall.

The cell itself was a study in holy overkill. The walls were "Blessed Granite"—stone that had been soaked in holy water for no less than six months, blessed by three different priests on three different holy days, and inscribed with wards that were supposed to suppress magical ability. The bars were silver—not silver-plated, but solid silver, because the Order never did anything by halves when it came to imprisoning people they considered threats.

The effect was that every breath Elara took tasted faintly of metal and sanctimony. Her skin itched where the holy air touched it, a constant low-grade irritation that was more annoying than painful. Like being forced to wear wool in summer while someone sang hymns slightly off-key in the background.

It certainly didn't help that the temperature was kept deliberately cold—another "feature" designed to make practitioners of death magic uncomfortable. Something about how necromancy thrived in warmth and rot, so naturally the Order kept their dungeons frigid enough to preserve meat.

Elara sat on the edge of the stone cot—a generous term for what was essentially a slab of rock with a blanket that had the texture and warmth of burlap—and swung her legs with affected nonchalance. She had spent the last hour using a stray bit of neon-pink magic to draw glowing caricatures of Sir Kaelen on the wall, testing the limits of the suppression wards.

Turns out, they were designed to stop big magic—resurrections, mass hauntings, the kind of flashy necromancy that got you executed instead of just imprisoned. Small-scale artistic defacement? That slipped right through.

In her drawings, Kaelen's chin was twice as large as life, his perpetually furrowed brow was three times as dramatic, and she'd given him a speech bubble that read "I AM VERY SERIOUS ABOUT JUSTICE" in wobbly letters.

It was petty. It was childish.

It made her feel minutely better about the seventeenth arrest.

The heavy iron door groaned open with the tortured shriek of metal on stone that the Order seemed to think added to the ambiance. Elara didn't look up immediately—that would imply she cared about who was visiting, and she had a reputation to maintain.

Kaelen stepped in, ducking his head to clear the low archway. He'd shed his cape and gauntlets since the arrest, but he was still wearing enough gold-plated armor to fund a small village for a year. Without the cape, she could see the way the armor fit him—perfectly tailored, every piece custom-made to accommodate his frankly unreasonable shoulders.

He looked tired. Not just "long night in a graveyard" tired, but "the weight of the world is leaning on my shoulders and I can feel my spine compressing" tired. There were new lines around his eyes, and his usually perfect posture had a slight slump to it that she'd never seen before.

Something had happened at the border. Something bad.

"The drawings are a nice touch," he said, his voice echoing in the small cell. He wasn't looking at the wall, but Elara saw his jaw twitch in that telltale way that meant he was fighting a smile. "Though I'd like to think my nose isn't quite that… angular."

"Art is subjective, Kaelen," Elara said, hopping off the cot with more energy than she felt. She walked toward the bars, her boots clicking on the damp floor, leaving muddy footprints that would probably scandalize the next priest who had to clean the cells. "So, is this the part where you tell me I'm being banished to the borderlands? Or are we skipping straight to the 'repent for your sins' lecture? Because I should warn you, I've heard the one about the 'corruption of the soul' at least four times this year alone. You really need new material."

Kaelen didn't answer immediately. He walked to the center of the small cell—three steps, that's all the room there was—and placed a heavy, leather-bound cylinder on the rickety wooden table that served as the cell's only furniture besides the cot.

When he looked at her, his eyes were dark, shadowed by something that looked uncomfortably close to fear.

Real fear. The kind that made seasoned paladins go quiet.

Elara's playful expression flickered. She knew Kaelen—knew him better than she probably should after three years of this dance. She knew his "I'm annoyed" face, his "I'm judging your life choices" face, his "I'm trying very hard not to laugh at your terrible jokes" face.

She'd never seen this face before. This was the face of a man who'd seen something that shook him to his foundation.

"We aren't banishing you, Elara," he said quietly, his voice pitched low enough that it wouldn't carry beyond the cell. "And I don't have the breath for a lecture."

The temperature in the cell seemed to drop another few degrees.

"Then why am I here?" Elara asked, and for once, there was no sarcasm in her voice. "Usually by now, you've given me a fine I cannot pay, a stern talking-to about 'respecting the sanctity of the grave,' and a very pointed suggestion to stay out of the Duke's backyard for at least a month."

"The Duke is the least of our problems."

Kaelen unrolled a map onto the table with hands that were perfectly steady despite the tension radiating from every line of his body. It was a map of the northern territories—Oakhaven at the bottom, marked with the sun-sigil of the Order, and stretching north for what looked like three hundred miles of increasingly wild territory before ending in the blank, unexplored reaches marked simply "The Grey Wastes."

"Three days ago," Kaelen said, his finger tracing a route on the map, "the village of northern Oakhaven—here, about a hundred miles north of the city—stopped responding to messengers."

Elara leaned forward, studying the geography. The northern Oakhaven was marked as the last "civilized" settlement before the true borderlands began. Beyond it, the map showed scattered hamlets, most without names, just dots indicating human presence in increasingly hostile terrain.

"Standard procedure," Kaelen continued. "We sent a scout. Fast rider, experienced tracker, blessed armor, holy wards. Everything by the book."

He paused, and Elara watched a muscle jump in his jaw.

"He returned this morning," Kaelen said, his voice carefully controlled. "Or rather, parts of him returned. Three-quarters of a man, Elara. The rest was just... gone. Not cut away. Not torn. Just absent, as if someone had taken an eraser to reality and selectively deleted portions of him."

Ice crawled up Elara's spine—and not the holy cold of the blessed granite. This was different. This was the crawling, instinctive cold of something fundamentally wrong with the world.

"And the parts that did come back," Kaelen said, reaching into a pouch at his belt, "were wrong."

He pulled out a small glass vial and set it on the table.

Inside was a clump of soil.

Elara had seen a lot of disturbing things in her years as a necromancer. Death in all its forms, decay in every stage, spirits so twisted by their manner of passing that they barely resembled the people they'd been.

But this soil made her skin crawl in a way she'd never experienced.

It was black. Not the rich, dark brown of good earth, not the ash-grey of burnt ground. This was a terrifying, absolute void-black—not merely the absence of light, but something that actively devoured it. The kind of black that hurt to look at directly, as if staring into it too long might let it stare back. Where the vial sat on the table, the air itself seemed dimmer, colors leaching away in a slow, creeping radius that made the blessed granite look dull and the silver bars appear tarnished.

"The void-rift," Elara whispered, the words tasting like ash in her mouth. "That's just a bedtime story. Something paladins tell squires to make them pray harder. 'Be good or the Void will eat your soul.'"

"It's real," Kaelen said, and the absolute conviction in his voice made her believe him instantly. "My Light couldn't touch it. I tried—

held my sword over this sample, channeled every bit of blessed power I could muster. The Light didn't repel it, didn't purify it. The darkness just… swallowed it. Consumed it like it was fuel."

He looked at her then, really looked at her, and Elara saw something she'd never expected to see in the eyes of the Golden Lion: helplessness.

"The High Priest's blessings did nothing," Kaelen continued, his voice rough. "The wards didn't hold. The prayers didn't work. Three entire villages are gone now, Elara. Not destroyed—erased. And it's spreading. The Rift is getting bigger."

He stepped closer to the bars until they were separated only by blessed silver and three years of complicated history.

"The High Order thinks that to fight a void of life, we need someone who understands the transition of it," he said. "They want a specialist. Someone who can speak to what's left behind when the living are gone. Someone who walks the line between life and death every single day."

Understanding crashed over Elara like a bucket of ice water.

"You want a necromancer," she said slowly. "The Golden Lion, paragon of the Order, wants to team up with the girl who uses 'foul arts' to find lost earrings and settle inheritance disputes?"

"I don't want to," Kaelen said, and the blunt honesty of it was almost refreshing. He stepped even closer, until his face was mere inches from the bars, close enough that she could see the gold flecks in his blue eyes. "I think this is a mistake. I think letting you out of this cell is an invitation to chaos. I think—"

He stopped, his throat working as he swallowed whatever he'd been about to say.

"But my men are dying, Elara," he said finally, his voice barely above a whisper. "Good men. Men with families. And the High Priest showed that sample to every practitioner in the city—healers, warlocks, blessed smiths, even a hedge witch who claims she can talk to trees. You're the only one who didn't look away when you saw it. You're the only one who didn't flinch."

Elara looked at the vial of void-black soil. She could feel it even from here—a wrongness that made her skin crawl and her magic curl in on itself protectively.

But Kaelen was right. She hadn't flinched. Because whatever that thing was, it wasn't natural. It wasn't part of the great cycle of life and death that governed her magic. It was an interruption. An erasure. An abomination.

And abominations, Elara had learned long ago, needed to be corrected.

"There's a catch," she said, her eyes moving from the vial to Kaelen's face. "There's always a catch with you people."

Kaelen reached into his belt and pulled out a pair of heavy iron manacles. But these weren't the crude shackles used for common prisoners. These were works of art—or horror, depending on your perspective. They were etched with glowing silver runes that hummed with a low, rhythmic vibration that Elara could feel in her bones.

Soul-binding runes.

"The High Priest won't let a criminal walk free in the Borderlands," Kaelen said, his voice strained in a way that told her he didn't like this any more than she did. "You go to the Rift. You help us close it. But you do it while tethered to me. Physically. Magically. Soul-bound. If you try to run, or if you try to use your magic for anything other than this mission—"

"The Warden's Link ritual," Elara interrupted, her eyes widening as true understanding hit. "Kaelen, that's... that's intimate. That's not just handcuffs. That's binding our life-forces together. If I die, you die. If you die, I die. And worse—we'll feel each other. Emotions. Pain. Eventually thoughts if the bond deepens enough."

She stepped back from the bars, her heart hammering in a way that had nothing to do with fear of the Void and everything to do with the implications of being magically handcuffed to the man she'd been mentally undressing for three years.

"That ritual is supposed to be for the worst criminals," she said, her voice pitching higher. "The ones too dangerous to kill but too powerful to contain. The ones—"

"I know what it's for," Kaelen cut her off. His face had gone slightly red, a flush creeping up his neck that was visible even in the terrible light. "The High Priest insisted. It was either this or leave you in the cell while the Borderlands burn."

Elara stared at him. At the manacles. At the vial of wrong-black soil that represented a threat she couldn't see but could feel in her bones.

Then she looked back at Kaelen—at the exhaustion in his eyes, at the weight he was carrying, at the fact that he'd come here himself instead of sending a lesser paladin to deliver the news.

She held her hands out through the bars, wrists together in a mockery of surrender.

"Well, Sir Kaelen," she said, her voice dropping back into that playful register even though her heart was racing, "if you wanted to be joined at the hip with me, you really could have just asked me for a dance at the Solstice Ball. This seems a bit extreme."

Kaelen's grip on the manacles tightened, his knuckles going white. When he spoke, his voice was rough with something that might have been frustration or might have been something far more complicated.

"Don't make me regret this, Elara."

She felt the cold metal close around her wrists, felt the runes beginning to activate with a warmth that spread up her arms, felt the first whisper of his presence at the edge of her consciousness.

"Oh, darling," she said, her eyes meeting his through the bars as the soul-bond began to take root. "I guarantee you're going to regret it. But at least you won't be bored."

Chapter Three

THE IMPOSSIBLE DEAL

The High Temple of Oakhaven was a masterclass in architectural arrogance.

Everything was white marble imported from quarries three hundred miles south, vaulted ceilings that soared so high they made normal human voices sound like the whispers of insects, and stained glass windows that depicted various saints doing very uncomfortable-looking things to demons. The message was clear: you are small, you are insignificant, and you should be very, very grateful that we allow you to exist in our magnificent presence.

For Elara, walking through the halls was like being a drop of ink in a vat of bleach. The sheer "holiness" of the air made her sinuses ache. Every surface had been blessed, every stone consecrated, every corner sanctified until the entire building radiated a low-grade hostility toward anything that smelled of death magic.

It was like walking into a building that was specifically designed to give her a migraine.

"Try not to look so... necro-y," Kaelen muttered, his hand firm but not painful on her elbow as he led her toward the Inner Sanctum. His armor clinked softly with each step, the sound echoing in the vast corridors.

"I'm wearing my best lace, Kaelen," Elara whispered back, gesturing at her admittedly muddy and somewhat tattered sleeves. "I even left the bone-dust at home. What more do you want from me? A hymn?"

"I want you to not provoke the High Priest within the first thirty seconds of meeting him."

"That's a very specific timeframe. Does that mean I can provoke him after thirty seconds?"

"Elara—"

"I'm joking. Mostly." She glanced at a particularly judgmental statue of a martyr holding what appeared to be his own intestines in one hand and a sword in the other. "But if one more priest looks at me like I'm a cockroach in the communion wine, I'm going to summon a spectral choir to sing bawdy tavern songs during their next prayer service."

"You will do no such thing," Kaelen growled, though his grip on her arm softened fractionally. Through the nascent bond between them—still forming, still fragile, but definitely there—she felt a flicker of what might have been reluctant amusement.

So he did have a sense of humor under all that golden righteousness. Good to know.

They passed through three separate checkpoints, each one manned by increasingly ornate guards who looked at Elara with expressions ranging from disgust to fascination. By the third checkpoint, she'd started waving cheerfully at them, which made Kaelen's jaw clench in that delightful way that told her she was getting under his skin.

The Inner Sanctum was less a room and more a statement of power. The floor was polished obsidian that reflected the light from a dozen floating mage-lights like a dark mirror. The walls were lined with relics under glass—bones of saints, fragments of supposedly holy artifacts, a collection of confiscated "dark magic" items that Elara suspected were mostly just party tricks and theatrical props.

And at the center of the room, standing behind a podium carved from a single piece of white quartz, stood High Priest Valerius.

He was a man who looked like he had been carved out of ancient, cold driftwood and then taught to stand upright through sheer force of will. His face was all sharp angles and deep-set eyes that held the kind of certainty that came from never, not once, questioning whether he might be wrong. His robes were white—so white they seemed to glow in the mage-light—and perfectly arranged without a single wrinkle or stain.

He didn't look at Elara when they entered. He looked through her, as if she were a particularly offensive smudge on the floor that someone would clean up eventually.

"Sir Kaelen," Valerius's voice was like dry parchment rubbing together. Each word was precise, clipped, drained of anything resembling warmth. "You are certain this... practitioner is necessary?"

The pause before "practitioner" was deliberate. Calculated to demean.

Elara felt Kaelen stiffen beside her. Through the bond, she felt his instant surge of anger—not at her, but on her behalf. It was so unexpected that she almost missed Kaelen's response.

"The scouts are returning as empty husks, Holiness," Kaelen said, his voice taking on a formal, rigid tone that Elara instinctively hated. This wasn't the gruff, exhausted man from the dungeon. This was the Golden Lion, perfect paladin, speaking to his superior. "My Light cannot navigate the rot. The blessed wards fail. The holy fire is consumed. Miss Vance's particular expertise may be our only option."

"May be," Valerius repeated, his thin lips compressing into an even thinner line. "That is not the language of certainty, Sir Kaelen. That is the language of desperation."

"Then I am desperate, Holiness."

The admission hung in the air like a confession. Valerius's eyes finally moved from the middle distance to actually look at Kaelen, and something flickered in those cold depths—satisfaction, perhaps, at seeing the mighty Lion humbled.

"Very well," the High Priest said after a long, uncomfortable pause. He turned his gaze to Elara for the first time, and the weight of his regard pressed on her like a physical thing. "The Warden's Link is a sacred rite, girl. It is usually reserved for the most dangerous of heretics—those too powerful to execute, too valuable to waste. If you stray too far from the Light of this Paladin, the thread will snap, and your soul will be... messy. Do you understand?"

Elara had prepared several responses. She'd had an entire sarcastic speech ready about soul-mates and cosmic irony and the universe's terrible sense of humor.

But something about the way Valerius said "messy"—as if her death would be an inconvenience he'd have to deal with, like spilled wine on an expensive carpet—killed the humor in her throat.

"I understand, Your Holiness," she said instead, keeping her voice carefully neutral.

Valerius's expression didn't change, but she saw the slight narrowing of his eyes. He'd expected defiance. Expected her to make this difficult.

Good. Let him be off-balance for once.

"Hands," Kaelen commanded, his voice dropping back into that professional, military clip.

Elara held out her wrists. Kaelen placed his own over hers, palms facing up. His hands were large enough to completely engulf hers, the skin rough with calluses from sword-work and scarred in places from battles she'd never witnessed. They were warrior's hands, but his touch was careful. Gentle, even.

His skin was hot—burning with the steady, banked fire of his holy vows. For a second, genuine nerves flickered through Elara. This wasn't just a spell. This wasn't a simple binding. This was a tether—a connection that would link her to another person in ways she'd never experienced, in ways that terrified her more than any void-rift.

She'd been alone for so long. Since her grandmother died. Since the village children threw stones. Since she'd built her armor of sarcasm and neon-pink defiance.

And now Kaelen would be inside that armor with her. Would feel what she felt. Would know what she kept hidden.

Through their joined hands, she felt his heartbeat. It was fast. Too fast for a man who appeared so calm.

He was nervous too.

Valerius began to chant in a language that sounded like clanging bells—Old Liturgical, the dead tongue of the Order's founders. Two acolytes stepped forward, carrying between them a basin of liquid silver that pulsed with a rhythmic, white light. The metal moved like living mercury, responding to the chant, rising and falling in gentle waves.

The High Priest dipped a fine brush into the silver and began to draw. Not on paper or parchment, but directly on their skin.

He started at Elara's right wrist and drew a continuous line that wrapped around her arm, crossed to Kaelen's left wrist, circled his forearm, and returned to her wrist to complete the circuit. The silver was cold—so cold it burned—and everywhere it touched, Elara's magic recoiled violently.

Her neon-pink power flared instinctively, trying to push the foreign magic away, trying to protect her from this invasion.

Kaelen's golden light rose to meet hers—but not to crush it. Not to smother it. His Light wrapped around her pink glow like a shield, like an embrace, containing her magic without destroying it.

The sensation was overwhelming. Intimate in a way that made her breath catch and her pulse skip. She could feel him now—not just his heartbeat, but his emotions. The steady thrum of duty. The exhaustion that went bone-deep. The sharp spike of concern for his men. And underneath it all, buried so deep he probably didn't even acknowledge it himself, a flicker of something that felt suspiciously like attraction.

Attraction he was trying very, very hard to smother.

Oh, Elara thought, her eyes widening slightly. So that's how it is.

Valerius's chanting reached a crescendo, and the silver line sank into their skin with a hiss of magic meeting flesh. It hurt—not a sharp pain, but a deep ache, like a bruise forming at high speed.

When it was done, all that remained was a faint, shimmering scar on both their wrists that looked like a thread of moonlight had been woven into their skin.

"It is done," Valerius declared, his brush clattering back into the basin. "Fifty feet, Sir Kaelen. Any further, and the girl's magic will implode. If she dies, you will feel the recoil—it will weaken you significantly, possibly permanently. If you die..." He looked at Elara with barely concealed disdain. "She will likely be executed anyway for failing her mission."

"Good to know the stakes are so balanced," Elara remarked, unable to help herself. Through the bond, she felt Kaelen's spike of alarm—not at Valerius, but worry for her. Worry that she'd just made herself a target.

The High Priest's eyes narrowed fractionally, but he didn't rise to the bait.

"Go," he said, dismissing them with a wave of his hand as if they were servants. "The Borderlands await. And girl?"

Elara paused at the doorway, looking back.

"Do try not to die too quickly," Valerius said with a smile that didn't reach his eyes. "It would be such a waste of Sir Kaelen's time."

Chapter Four

THE TETHER

By the time they reached the Cathedral gates, Kaelen's warhorse was waiting with the patient, long-suffering expression of an animal who had seen too much and expected nothing good.

Cinder was seventeen hands of solid muscle and bad attitude, his charcoal coat scarred from a dozen campaigns. He took one look at Elara's neon-pink aura and pinned his ears flat against his skull.

"The horse hates me," Elara observed.

"Cinder doesn't hate anyone," Kaelen said. "He's just discerning."

"That's a diplomatic way of saying I smell like a graveyard."

"You were literally digging in one two hours ago."

The banter died as they approached the mounting block. The reality of what was about to happen—days on the road, tethered together, forced into proximity that neither of them had agreed to—settled over them like a heavy cloak.

"One horse?" Elara asked, her usual sarcasm tinged with genuine uncertainty.

Kaelen looked at her, and through the nascent bond between them, she felt his conflict. Part of him—the part that followed orders, that believed in the mission—saw the logic. The tether required proximity. One horse made sense.

Another part of him, buried deeper, was acutely aware of what it would mean to have her pressed against his back for days. To feel her breath on his neck, her arms around his waist, the warmth of her despite the cold metal of his armor.

"Cinder has a long stride," Kaelen said, his voice carefully neutral. "If you fall more than fifty feet behind, the tether snaps. You die. I don't recommend it."

Elara held out her hand, and he pulled her up behind him in one smooth motion. The moment she settled onto the saddle, her chest pressed against his backplate, the silver tether hummed with acknowledgment.

Too close. This was far too close.

"Comfortable?" Kaelen asked, his voice rougher than intended.

"Immensely," Elara lied, wrapping her arms around his waist. Through the armor, she could feel the tension in him—the way every muscle was locked tight, as if he was bracing for battle. "Though I should warn you, I'm going to complain the entire way to the Borderlands."

"You're already complaining."

"I'm just getting started, darling."

Kaelen gave Cinder the signal, and they rode through the gates as the sun set over Oakhaven. Behind them, the Cathedral bells tolled evening prayers. Ahead, the sky grew darker with each mile, the Borderlands waiting with their secrets and their void-rifts and the truth that would change everything.

The silver tether pulsed between them, a constant reminder that for better or worse, they were bound now. Fifty feet or death.

Kaelen suspected that death might be the easier option.

· · ·

They rode in silence for the first hour, the rhythm of Cinder's hooves the only sound besides the wind through the autumn trees. The well-maintained roads around Oakhaven gave way to packed dirt paths as they traveled north, and the farms that dotted the landscape became sparser with each passing mile.

Elara shifted behind him, trying to find a position that didn't make her back ache or her legs cramp. Riding wasn't her forte—she spent most of her time in graveyards, not on horseback—and the awkwardness of sharing a saddle with someone wearing fifty pounds of armor wasn't helping.

"You're going to fall off if you keep fidgeting," Kaelen said without looking back.

"I'm not fidgeting. I'm adjusting. There's a difference."

"You've 'adjusted' six times in the last ten minutes."

"Well, excuse me for not being used to riding behind a mobile fortress. Do you sleep in that armor too? Because that would explain so much about your personality."

Through the bond, she felt a flicker of amusement, quickly suppressed.

"I don't sleep in the armor," he said.

"Do you ever take it off?"

"When necessary."

"Define necessary."

"When I need to bathe. When it requires maintenance. When..." He paused, and Elara felt something shift in the bond—a memory surfacing, old and sharp. "When someone needs to tend a wound."

The way he said it—flat, automatic—made Elara pay attention.

"Speaking from experience?" she asked, keeping her tone light despite the sudden tension she felt radiating from him.

"Every paladin has scars," Kaelen said. "It's part of the training."

"Training scars are usually small. Controlled. Accidents that teach you to keep your guard up." Elara leaned slightly to the side, trying to see his face. "You make it sound like yours are... different."

For a long moment, Kaelen didn't respond. The only sound was Cinder's steady gait and the wind rustling through the trees. Then, without ceremony or preamble, he began unbuckling his right vambrace.

"What are you doing?" Elara asked, startled.

"Showing you different."

He pulled the armored sleeve off and extended his right arm slightly to the side, where she could see it. Even in the fading light, the scar was visible—a long, puckered line that ran from just below his elbow halfway to his wrist. It looked like it had been made by a training blade that went too deep, the kind of wound that should have been carefully tended but instead had been allowed to heal rough.

"Berenger," Kaelen said quietly, his voice carefully neutral. "When I was twelve. I dropped my guard during a drill. He said the scar would remind me that hesitation kills."

Elara's eyes traced the old wound, and through the bond, she felt the complicated knot of emotions tied to that memory. Pride and shame and a desperate need for approval all tangled together.

"He cut you," she said slowly. "Your teacher cut you. On purpose."

"He corrected me," Kaelen said, his thumb tracing the old wound absently—a gesture so practiced it seemed unconscious. "I made a mistake. Hesitated when I should have struck. In real combat, that hesitation would have gotten me killed. Berenger made sure I understood the consequences."

"You were twelve."

"I was training to be a paladin. Age doesn't matter when you're learning to survive."

Elara stared at the scar, at the way Kaelen's thumb kept moving over it as if seeking comfort from the very thing that had hurt him. Through the bond, she could feel his certainty—his absolute conviction that this had been necessary, that Berenger had done him a favor, that the pain had been a gift.

It made her chest tighten in a way that had nothing to do with the tether.

"Did he apologize?" she asked before she could stop herself.

Kaelen looked genuinely confused by the question. "Why would he apologize? I made the mistake. He corrected it. That's what mentors do."

"Kaelen…" Elara chose her words carefully. "Mentors aren't supposed to scar children. Correction shouldn't require bloodshed."

"It wasn't bloodshed. It was a lesson." He pulled his arm back and began re-buckling the vambrace, his movements precise and practiced. "Berenger taught me everything I know about being a paladin. Everything about duty, sacrifice, discipline. He made me strong."

"He made you afraid to hesitate," Elara said quietly.

Through the bond, she felt Kaelen's immediate defensiveness, followed by a flicker of something that might have been doubt. But he buried it quickly, the way he buried everything that didn't fit neatly into his worldview.

"I'm alive because of his lessons," Kaelen said firmly. "I've survived battles that killed better men because I don't hesitate. I don't second-guess. I act. That's what he taught me."

Elara wanted to argue. Wanted to tell him that survival purchased at the cost of your humanity wasn't really survival at all. That a teacher who left scars on a twelve-year-old boy wasn't teaching—he was breaking.

But she could feel Kaelen's walls going up, the bond suddenly feeling more distant as he retreated into the certainty of his training.

So instead, she did something she almost never did.

She let it go.

"I'm sorry you were hurt," she said. "Even if you think it was necessary. I'm sorry you were twelve years old and scared and alone, and the person who was supposed to protect you hurt you instead."

Kaelen went motionless. Through the bond, she felt shock, then a wave of something raw and painful that he immediately tried to suppress.

"I wasn't alone," he said, but his voice had gone rough. "I had the Order. I had my brothers. I had—"

"You were twelve, Kaelen," Elara interrupted gently. "And you were scared. The bond doesn't lie. I can feel it. That little boy who held still while his mentor cut him open—he was terrified. And he thought he deserved it."

"Elara—"

"You don't have to talk about it," she said, sensing his distress. "I just... I wanted you to know that someone sees it. Sees what was done to you. And thinks it was wrong."

Silence fell between them again, but it was different now. Heavier. The bond thrummed with emotions neither of them wanted to name.

Finally, Kaelen spoke, his voice so quiet she almost missed it.

"He told me I'd finally become the son he should have had. That my father would be ashamed of what he'd been—a coward who put mercy above duty—but that I'd redeemed the family name by becoming everything he wasn't."

Through the bond, Elara felt the weight of that statement. The pride and the pain. The desperate need for approval from a man who had weaponized love and called it teaching.

She didn't say anything. Just tightened her arms around his waist slightly—a small gesture of comfort that she hoped said what words couldn't.

They rode on into the deepening dusk, the silver tether pulsing between them, binding them together in ways that had nothing to do with magic and everything to do with the slow, painful process of being seen.

Chapter Five

LEAVING OAKHAVEN

Their first journey on the road began in silence.

They'd been riding north for twelve hours straight, covering what Kaelen estimated was nearly forty miles. At this pace, they'd reach the Silent Woods by tomorrow evening, Blackpine Keep by the third day if Cinder held up. The northern Oakhaven—the village that had gone silent—was still two days beyond that, deep into territory where the Order's influence was more theoretical than practical.

The landscape around Oakhaven was familiar territory—rolling hills dotted with farms, orchards heavy with late summer fruit, small villages where children played in the dusty streets and farmers waved at passing travelers. This was the heartland of the Order's influence, where every crossroads had a shrine and every inn displayed the sun-sigil with pride.

Elara watched the landscape change as they traveled. The well-maintained roads around Oakhaven gave way to packed dirt paths, then to barely-visible game trails. Farms became sparse, then disappeared entirely. The further north they went, the more the world felt like it was holding its breath.

It was also, she realized with growing unease, completely devoid of ghosts.

Normally, traveling through populated areas meant navigating a constant stream of spectral presence. Ancestors lingering near family homes, spirits of travelers who'd died on the road, the occasional confused ghost who hadn't realized they were dead yet. It was like background noise for a necromancer—always there, always humming at the edge of perception.

Here, there was nothing. The Order's consecration was absolute.

"It's too quiet," Elara murmured against Kaelen's back.

"We're barely ten miles from the city," Kaelen replied. "What were you expecting? Bandits?"

"I was expecting the dead," she said. "There should be thousands of them. This is farmland—people have lived and died here for centuries. But I cannot feel a single spirit. It's like they've all been… erased."

Through the tether, Kaelen felt her discomfort shift into something sharper. Fear, maybe, or recognition of something fundamentally wrong.

"The Order consecrates the major roads," he said, though even to his own ears it sounded like an excuse. "It's supposed to provide safe passage for travelers. Keep malevolent spirits at bay."

"Malevolent spirits are rare, Kaelen. Most ghosts just want someone to listen. By 'keeping them at bay,' your Order is silencing them. Making them invisible." She paused. "Making them forgotten."

He had no response to that. What could he say? That it was necessary? That the dead had no rights? That the living needed protection from the very idea of mortality?

Three weeks ago, he would have said all of those things without hesitation. Now, with Elara's arms around his waist and her magic humming against his awareness through the tether, the certainties felt less certain.

Cinder's ears suddenly swiveled forward, and the warhorse's entire body went rigid beneath them.

"What is it, boy?" Kaelen's hand went to his sword hilt instinctively.

Then Elara felt it too—a presence, but not a living one. A spirit, strong and angry, manifesting directly in front of them on the road.

It was a translucent figure in ancient armor, its spectral form flickering with barely contained rage. Not one of Elara's carefully managed clients, but a wild ghost—unbound, unconsecrated, existing in direct defiance of the Order's laws.

Cinder reared, his hooves lashing out at the ghost with a horse's instinctive fear of the unnatural. Kaelen fought to control him, his thighs clamping tight to the saddle as the warhorse bucked and spun.

"Easy! Cinder, stand down!"

But the horse was beyond reason, his eyes rolling white as the ghost advanced.

"Let me handle this," Elara said, sliding off the horse before Kaelen could stop her. The tether stretched taut between them as she put distance between herself and the panicking animal.

She approached the ghost with her hands raised, palms out, her magic flaring pink in greeting rather than threat.

"Peace," she said quietly. "I'm not here to banish you. What's your name?"

The ghost's rage flickered, confusion replacing fury. When was the last time anyone had asked his name?

"Marcus," the spirit said, his voice like wind through dead leaves. "Marcus of the Fourth Legion. I died on this road three hundred years ago, and I've been trying to warn travelers ever since. But they cannot hear me. They cannot see me. Until you."

"Warn them about what?" Elara asked.

"The Light," Marcus said, and his spectral hand pointed north, toward the Borderlands. "The Light is wrong. It's eating the darkness, and without darkness, there can be no rest. The dead are being erased, necromancer. And no one is listening."

Elara's blood ran cold. "I'm listening now," she said softly. "Tell me everything."

Behind her, Kaelen watched as Elara conducted a conversation with empty air. Through the tether, he could feel her focus, her compassion, her absolute certainty that what she was doing mattered.

And Cinder, despite his fear, despite every instinct telling him to run, stood perfectly still.

Because even a warhorse could sense that this moment was important.

That something fundamental was shifting in the world.

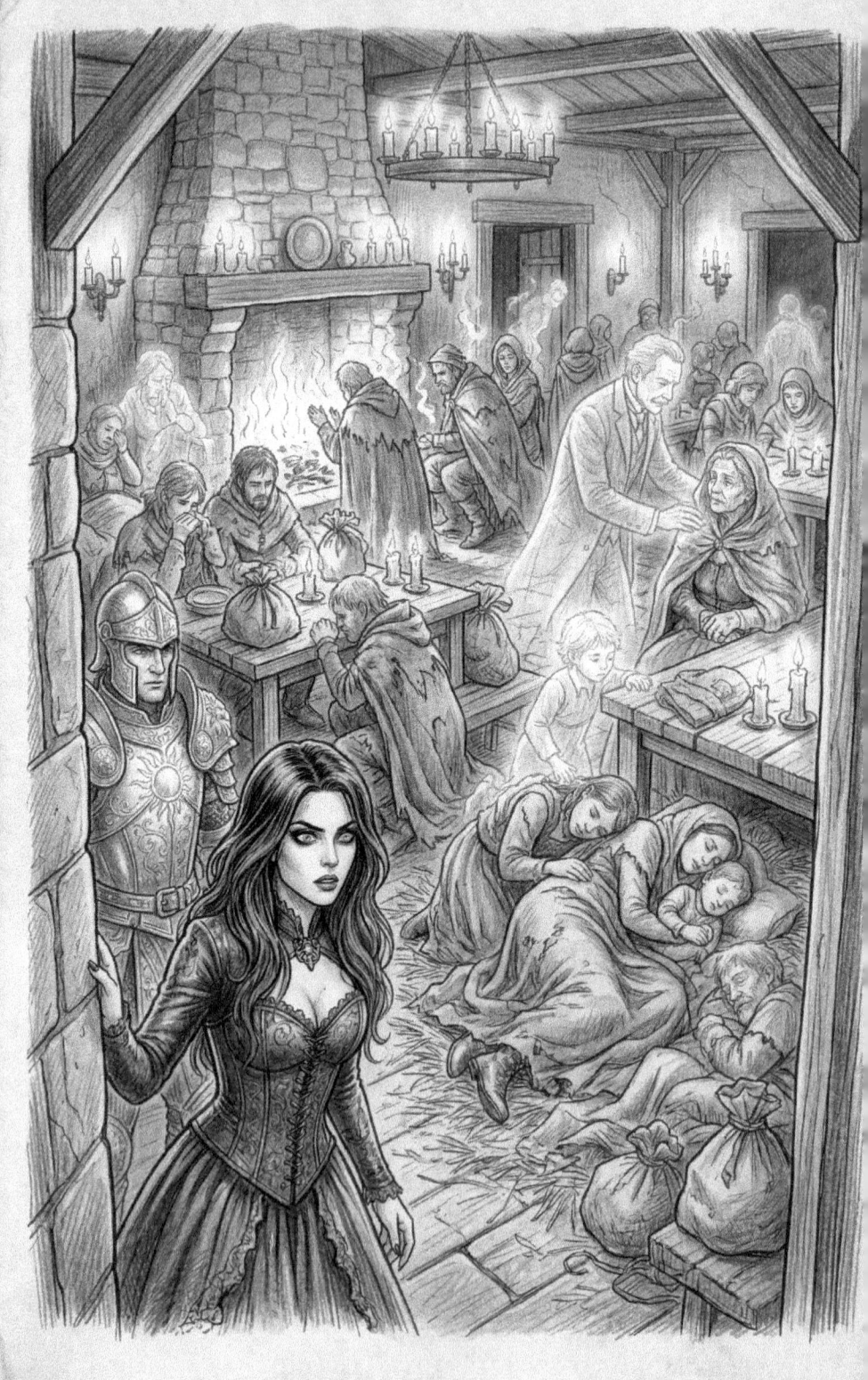

Chapter Six

THE FIRST INN

The Rusty Lantern appeared on the horizon like a promise of civilization in an increasingly wild landscape.

They'd been riding for twelve hours straight, stopping only to water Cinder and let Elara stretch her legs enough that the tether didn't pull painfully tight. The sun had set two hours ago, and the temperature had dropped with the particular viciousness of early autumn nights in the borderlands.

Elara was shivering despite being pressed against Kaelen's back. Her lace sleeves, so dramatic and lovely in Oakhaven's graveyards, provided approximately zero protection against the wind. Her fingers were numb where they gripped Kaelen's belt, and she was quite certain that hypothermia was a real and present danger.

"Almost there," Kaelen said, and through the tether she felt his concern for her. He'd been monitoring her temperature drop through their connection, feeling the way her shivering had progressed from mild to concerning.

"If I freeze to death, does the tether snap before or after rigor mortis sets in?" Elara's teeth chattered. "Asking for a friend."

"You're not going to freeze to death."

"Easy for you to say. You're wrapped in a personal furnace of holy righteousness. I'm wearing decorative lace."

"I noticed."

The dry tone made her laugh despite the cold, and through the bond, she felt his satisfaction at having distracted her from her discomfort, even briefly.

. . .

The inn was packed—refugees from the northern villages, all fleeing south with whatever they could carry. The common room smelled of wet wool, fear, and the particular desperation of people who'd left everything behind.

Elara felt them before she saw them: the ghosts. Dozens of them, clustered around their living families, trying desperately to be seen, to be heard, to offer comfort that would never reach its destination. A spectral woman sat beside a weeping child, her translucent hand passing through the girl's hair over and over in a gesture of comfort that the living couldn't feel. An old man's ghost stood in the corner, watching his son argue with the innkeeper about the price of a room, trying to interject advice that would never be heard.

"They're all here," Elara whispered. "The dead. They followed their families south."

Through the tether, Kaelen felt her grief, her helplessness. She could see them, could hear their pleas for help, but with the tether suppressing her magic and fifty refugees watching, there was nothing she could do.

"Later," Kaelen said quietly, understanding without her needing to explain. "When we're alone, you can help them. I won't stop you."

The promise, small as it was, made something warm bloom in her chest.

The innkeeper's face went pale when he saw Kaelen's armor, paler still when he noticed the silver tether connecting the paladin to the dark-haired woman behind him—though even in the lamplight, he could see the strange pink streaks threaded through her brown hair, faintly luminous, like something that didn't belong to nature.

"One room," Kaelen said, his voice allowing no argument. "Private. Secure."

"My lord, I… there's only the attic left. And it's just the one bed—"

"We'll take it."

Elara felt Kaelen's resignation through the bond. He'd known this was coming. Had probably been dreading it since they left Oakhaven. The logistics of the tether meant they couldn't sleep in separate rooms. Could barely sleep in separate beds. The fifty-foot rule was absolute.

The innkeeper's eyes darted between them, clearly trying to determine the nature of their relationship. Prisoner and captor? Lovers? Something more complicated?

All of the above, Elara thought wryly, and felt Kaelen's spike of alarm through the bond as he caught the edge of her thought.

"Just the room," Kaelen said firmly, cutting off whatever speculation the innkeeper was brewing.

*   *   *

The attic was small, sloped, barely tall enough for Kaelen to stand upright. A single narrow bed dominated the space, and in the corner, steam rose from a copper bathing tub that looked like it had been hauled up three flights of stairs with great difficulty and minimal enthusiasm.

"One tub too," the innkeeper had said apologetically. "The hearth is full. Can't heat water for two."

Now, standing in the cramped space with Kaelen, the reality of their situation hit Elara with full force.

They were going to have to share everything. Space. Air. Water. The boundary between them was already blurred by the soul-bond, and now physical proximity was going to blur it even further.

"I'll take the floor," Kaelen said immediately, his eyes fixed on a point somewhere over her left shoulder.

"In full armor? You'll destroy your back."

"I'm fine."

"You're not fine. You're exhausted, you haven't slept properly in three days, and if you don't rest tonight, you'll be useless tomorrow when we actually need you." Elara started unlacing her boots, her frozen fingers fumbling with the knots. "We'll share the bed. Like adults. With a bolster between us for your delicate sensibilities."

"Elara—"

"Take off the armor, Kaelen."

Through the tether, she felt his conflict. The Order's rules said he couldn't disarm in front of a prisoner. His body said he desperately needed to rest. And somewhere, buried deep, a part of him that he refused to acknowledge wanted to see what it would feel like to sleep beside her without the metal wall between them.

"Turn around," he said finally.

Elara turned, presenting him with her back. She heard the methodical clink of buckles being undone, the heavy thud of plate hitting the floor. Each piece falling away like layers of identity being shed.

The sounds were intimate in a way that had nothing to do with nudity and everything to do with vulnerability. She was hearing Kaelen dismantle the armor he'd worn since he was fifteen. The golden shell that made him the "Lion," the symbol, the legend.

When she turned back, Kaelen stood in a simple linen tunic and trousers, his feet bare, his hair disheveled from being trapped under his helm all day. Without the armor, he looked younger. More human. More vulnerable.

There was a scar on his right forearm—the one Berenger had given him. She'd seen it earlier on the road, but now, in the soft lamplight of the attic, she could see others. A pale line across his collarbone. Burn marks on his left shoulder that looked like they'd come from holy fire gone wrong. The faint traces of dozens of smaller wounds that had healed but left their mark.

Kaelen caught her looking and crossed his arms self-consciously.

"Your turn," he said, gesturing to the tub. "I'll face the wall."

"The water's going to get cold if we take turns," Elara pointed out, then saw his expression and laughed. "Relax, darling. I meant I'll bathe first, quickly, so you can have it while it's still warm. I wasn't suggesting we share. Your virtue is safe."

"I'm not worried about my virtue," Kaelen muttered, but his ears had gone slightly red.

Through the bond, Elara felt his acute awareness of her, the effort it was taking him to think about literally anything else, and the growing realization that the tether was making privacy impossible in ways that had nothing to do with physical proximity.

She could feel what he felt. And he could feel what she felt. And right now, what they both felt was a deeply inconvenient attraction that was getting harder to ignore with every passing hour.

"Wall. Now," Elara commanded, pointing.

Kaelen turned obediently, and she heard him start reciting what sounded like a prayer under his breath—probably trying to distract himself.

They managed it with surprising efficiency—the awkward dance of two people trying very hard not to see each other naked while bound by a magical tether that transmitted every spike of awareness, every flutter of attraction, every moment of wanting what they absolutely should not want.

Elara stripped quickly and sank into the copper tub with a sigh of relief that was probably more audible than it should have been. The hot water on her frozen skin felt like heaven, and she couldn't quite suppress the small sound of pleasure that escaped her throat.

Through the bond, she felt Kaelen's reaction—a spike of heat followed by intense concentration on... was he counting in Old Liturgical? Oh, he absolutely was.

"You can stop reciting the prayer of chastity," she called over her shoulder, grinning despite herself. "I promise I'm not trying to seduce you with my bathing sounds."

"I'm not—" He stopped. "How did you know what I was reciting?"

"The tether works both ways, remember? I can feel you trying very hard to think pure thoughts."

"This was a terrible idea," Kaelen said, but there was a note of resignation in his voice that suggested he'd already known it would be.

"The tether or the mission?"

"Both. Neither. I don't know anymore."

Elara finished washing quickly—partially out of consideration for Kaelen's clearly fraying composure, partially because the water was already cooling. She stepped out, wrapped herself in the rough linen towel the innkeeper had provided, and pulled on the clean shift she'd stuffed into her pack before leaving Oakhaven.

"Your turn," she said, moving to the far corner of the room. "I'll face the wall this time. Fair is fair."

She heard him move, heard the soft splash as he got into the tub, heard his sharp intake of breath at the temperature.

"Still warm?" she asked.

"Barely. But better than nothing."

They were quiet for a while, the only sound the occasional splash of water and the muffled noise from the common room below. Through the tether, Elara could feel Kaelen's exhaustion seeping into relaxation as the hot water worked on his sore muscles.

"Thank you," he said quietly.

"For what?"

"For not making this harder than it already is."

Elara smiled at the wall. "The night is young, Kaelen. I make no promises about tomorrow."

She heard his huff of what might have been laughter.

◦ ◦ ◦

By the time they both climbed into the narrow bed, separated by a bolster that was more symbolic than effective, Elara was clean, warm, and acutely aware of every inch of Kaelen's body mere feet from hers.

The bed was absurdly small. Meant for one person, maybe a married couple who didn't mind being pressed together. For two people trying to maintain professional distance while magically bound? It was a joke.

They lay rigidly on their respective sides of the bolster, both staring at the ceiling, both hyperaware of the other's presence.

"This is fine," Elara said to the darkness.

"Completely fine," Kaelen agreed.

Through the bond, they both knew the other was lying.

"Goodnight, Kaelen," she whispered.

"Goodnight, Elara."

Silence fell, but it wasn't the comfortable kind. It was the loaded silence of two people trying not to think about what they were thinking about, which of course made them think about it more.

Through the tether, she felt him trying not to think about her. Felt him failing. Felt the way his awareness kept drifting to the warmth of her so close, the scent of the soap they'd both used, the soft sound of her breathing.

And she knew he could feel the same from her. The way her pulse had picked up. The way she was acutely conscious of the bare six inches separating them.

"Kaelen?" she whispered after several long minutes.

"Hmm?"

"This is going to be a very long journey, isn't it?"

She felt his rueful agreement through the bond. "Yes. Yes, it is."

And despite everything—the Void, the mission, the danger waiting ahead—Elara smiled into the darkness.

This was going to be an interesting journey indeed.

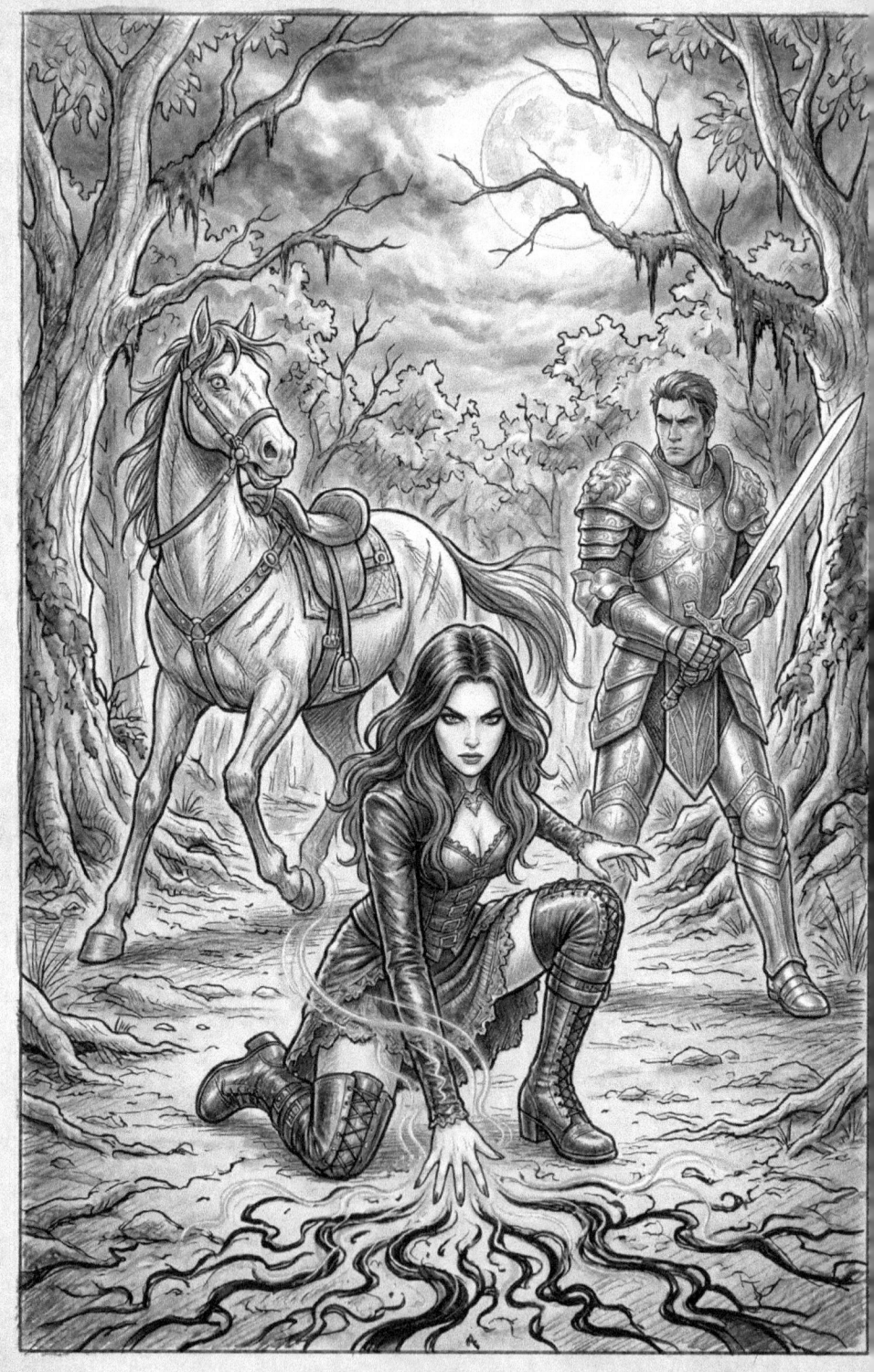

Chapter Seven

SKIRMISH IN THE DARK

The morning brought no sun.

By the third day of their journey, the sky had transformed from its usual blue to a sickly, bruised purple that made everything look like it was underwater. The light was wrong—flat and dim despite the fact that it was supposed to be midday. Birds didn't sing. The wind had a smell to it that Elara couldn't quite place but that made her magic curl in on itself protectively.

They were getting close to the void-rift.

Cinder felt it too. The warhorse had gone from his usual grudging tolerance of Elara's presence to active nervousness, his ears swiveling constantly, his stride choppy and uncertain. Twice he'd shied at nothing, forcing Kaelen to spend several minutes calming him.

"Easy, boy," Kaelen murmured, running a hand down the horse's neck. "We're not there yet."

"How can you tell?" Elara asked from her position behind him. She'd grown accustomed to the rhythm of riding with Kaelen—the way his back moved with each of Cinder's steps, the warmth of him even through the armor, the steady thrum of the tether connecting them.

"The trees are still green," Kaelen said, gesturing to the forest that lined the road. "Once we cross into the affected zone, the color drains. Everything turns grey first, then black, then it just... crumbles to soot."

Elara looked at the trees. They were green, but it was a sickly, faded green—like plants that weren't getting enough water, that were struggling to survive in soil that had gone bad.

"Kaelen," she said quietly, "I need you to stop for a moment."

He pulled Cinder to a halt immediately, his hand going to his sword hilt. "What's wrong?"

"Nothing's wrong. I just need to check something." She slid off the horse, her boots hitting the packed earth with a soft thud. The moment her feet touched the ground, she felt it.

The earth was sick.

Elara had spent her entire life with one foot in the grave, metaphorically speaking. She could sense the health of the soil the way a farmer could read the weather—it was part of her magic, part of her connection to the cycle of life and death. Good earth felt alive, thrumming with the slow, patient energy of decomposition and renewal. It welcomed the dead, transformed them, gave them back to the world as nutrients and growth.

This earth felt hollow. Empty. Like something had reached down and scooped out all the life, leaving only a shell.

She knelt, pressing her palm flat against the ground. Her magic flowed out instinctively, seeking, searching for the network of death and rebirth that should be everywhere—insects, small animals, plants, all the tiny deaths that fed the cycle.

There was nothing.

Not dead. Not alive. Just... absent.

"Elara?" Kaelen's voice was tight with concern. He'd dismounted and was standing beside her, one hand on her shoulder. "What do you feel?"

"Nothing," she whispered, pulling her hand back as if the ground had burned her. "I feel nothing, Kaelen. The earth is supposed to sing with death—it's natural, it's necessary, it's the foundation of everything. But this... this is silence. Complete silence."

"The Void," Kaelen said, his jaw clenching.

"It's not here yet—not fully. But it's close. Whatever this thing is, it's eating the death before it can complete the cycle. It's stealing the Life-Debt before it can be paid."

She stood, brushing the dirt from her hands, and that's when she heard it.

A sound that was not quite a sob, not quite a scream. A wet, choking noise that came from somewhere in the trees to their left.

Kaelen's sword was drawn before Elara could blink, the silver blade catching what little light filtered through the purple sky. Through the tether, she felt his combat readiness—the way his entire body shifted into a stance she recognized from watching him in the Cathedral courtyard during training exercises.

"Stay behind me," he commanded, his voice dropping into that military register that brooked no argument.

"Kaelen, wait—"

The thing that stumbled out of the trees was not a monster. Or rather, it had been a deer once. A young buck, judging by the small antlers.

But the corruption had transformed it into something that made Elara's stomach turn.

Half of its body was still organic—fur and bone and muscle, tawny brown and trembling. But the other half was being actively consumed by the void-corruption, and watching it happen was like watching reality itself dissolve.

The blackness wasn't spreading like a stain or an infection. It was spreading like cellular dissolution—Elara could see individual patches of fur and flesh turning translucent at the edges, the boundaries between solid matter and void becoming uncertain, wavering. The corruption had a texture like oil on water, shifting between absolute darkness and a disturbing semi-transparency that revealed the deer's internal structure breaking down, bones becoming visible through meat that was losing its opacity.

Where the void touched, color didn't just drain—it inverted, creating patches of negative space that hurt to look at directly. The deer's flank rippled with spreading fractal patterns, each branch of corruption subdividing into smaller and smaller iterations until the detail became too fine for the eye to track. It looked less like decay and more like reality was being unwritten, one pixel at a time.

Where the creature should have had eyes, there were glowing, jagged cracks in its skull that bled shadow. Literal shadow—not darkness, but the absence of light made manifest, spilling out like smoke, like blood, like something that shouldn't exist in three-dimensional space.

The transitions between flesh and void were the worst part—there was no clean line, no clear boundary. Instead, the deer's body seemed to exist in multiple states simultaneously at those edges: solid and liquid and something else entirely, all occupying the same space, all equally real and equally wrong.

It lunged.

Kaelen reacted on instinct. He swung his sword in a massive, horizontal arc, and the blade erupted in brilliant, sun-bright gold as he channeled his Holy Light into the strike.

It should have cleaved the corrupted deer in two. It should have purified the darkness, burned away the Void, restored the natural order.

Instead, the golden light hit the black mass and was absorbed. Swallowed whole. The deer-thing didn't even flinch—it simply inhaled the Light like a starving man at a feast, the cracks in its skull glowing brighter as it fed.

"What—" Kaelen staggered back, his sword dimming in his hands. Through the tether, Elara felt his shock, his disbelief, his dawning horror as the weapon he'd relied on his entire life proved utterly useless.

The creature reared up, its shadow-claws reaching for Kaelen's throat, moving with unnatural speed—

"Move, you shiny idiot!" Elara screamed.

She didn't use a spell. She didn't have time for the careful, respectful necromancy she usually practiced. She used a Command— the kind of raw, primal magic that reached down into the bones of the world and demanded obedience.

She slammed her hand into the ground, and her magic didn't glow pink. It turned a sharp, violent violet—the color of bruises, of storms, of power that was dangerous and barely controlled.

"Return what is borrowed!" she shrieked, her voice layered with harmonics that didn't sound entirely human.

A skeletal hand—massive, ancient, wrong—erupted from the dirt directly beneath the deer-thing. It wasn't the deer's skeleton; it was something older, something that had been sleeping in this soil long before the roads were built. The memory of a bear, perhaps, or something larger. The earth had recalled it at Elara's command, and it was angry at being disturbed.

The skeletal claws clamped shut around the shadow-deer with bone-crushing force, dragging it down into the earth. The creature screeched—a sound that made Elara's ears ring and her magic recoil—and then it was gone, swallowed by the soil.

The bear-bones crumbled back into dust, their purpose fulfilled.

Silence fell over the forest—the oppressive, wrong silence that came from too much death in one place.

Kaelen stood panting, his sword trembling in his hand. He looked at the spot where the creature had been, then at Elara, who was white as a sheet, her hands shaking as she wiped the violet sparks from her palms.

"You saved me," Kaelen said, his voice barely a whisper.

"I saved my tether," Elara snapped, though her voice lacked its usual sting. Through the bond, he could feel her lie—could feel the terror she'd felt when that thing had lunged for him, the absolute refusal to let him die. "If you die, I explode, remember? I'm very invested in your continued breathing."

Kaelen walked over to her slowly, like he was approaching a spooked horse. He sheathed his sword—useless thing that it had proven to be—and reached out, his hand gentle as he brushed a stray bit of grey soot from her cheek. His touch lingered, warm against her cold skin, and for a second the terrifying world seemed to recede.

"The High Priest said your magic was a rot," Kaelen said quietly, his blue eyes searching hers with an intensity that made her breath catch. "But that thing... that thing was the rot. You were the only thing that stopped it."

Elara swallowed hard. The banter was gone, stripped away by the reality of what they'd just faced. The wall she'd built with jokes and sarcasm was cracking, and Kaelen could see through to the frightened woman underneath—the one who'd just realized that the Void was worse than anything she'd imagined.

"Get back on the horse, Kaelen," she said softly, her voice steadier than she felt. "Before I start thinking you actually like me."

"We have work to do," he said, but he didn't deny it. Didn't pull away from her. His hand remained on her cheek for another heartbeat, his thumb brushing against her skin in a gesture that was far too intimate for a warden and his prisoner.

Then he stepped back, offering her his hand to help her mount Cinder.

As they rode away from the site of the skirmish, Elara pressed against Kaelen's back and tried not to think about the fact that his Holy Light—the thing he'd spent his entire life believing was the answer to every darkness—had failed.

And her magic—the thing he'd spent his entire life hunting as corruption—had been the only thing that worked.

The world was more complicated than either of them had been taught. And the Void was waiting ahead, hungry and patient, ready to prove just how insufficient all their certainties really were.

Chapter Eight

THE VILLAGE OF SILENCES

The "Silent Woods" were aptly named, but not for the reasons Kaelen had expected.

It wasn't just the lack of birdsong or the way the wind seemed to die the moment they stepped beneath the canopy of ash-grey trees. It was the weight of the silence. It was a physical thing, pressing against his eardrums, settling on his shoulders like a leaden cloak, demanding a reverence he usually reserved for the High Cathedral.

The forest itself seemed wrong. The trees were ancient—trunks wider than houses, roots that erupted from the soil in gnarled tangles—but their leaves had a sickly, translucent quality, as if they were only half-present in the world. The light that filtered through the canopy was dim and greenish, turning everything into an underwater tableau.

"Kaelen," Elara whispered, her voice muffled as if the woods were trying to swallow the sound whole. "I feel it."

"Feel what?"

"Them. Hundreds of them. Maybe thousands." Her hands tightened on his waist. "They're trapped, Kaelen. The spirits here—they're caught between. Not alive, not properly dead. Just... lingering."

They reached the village at the heart of the woods just as the pale, sickly sun began to dip below the horizon. The settlement was eerily intact—no burned roofs, no blood in the streets, no signs of violence. Laundry still hung on lines, tools leaned against barn walls, a child's wooden toy lay abandoned in the middle of the road.

And everywhere—standing in doorways, sitting on porches, leaning against garden fences—were people.

They weren't moving. They weren't breathing.

But they weren't corpses, either.

Elara slid off Cinder before Kaelen could stop her, the silver tether pulling taut as she approached the nearest figure—a young woman frozen mid-step, her hand reaching for a well bucket she would never grasp.

"Her soul is still inside," Elara breathed, her neon-pink magic flaring as she examined the woman. Through the tether, Kaelen felt her horror, her grief, her fury at what had been done here. "They're all still inside. Trapped in their own bodies like... like insects in amber."

Kaelen dismounted, his golden armor clanking in the oppressive silence. He approached an old man sitting on a bench, his face frozen in an expression of mild curiosity, as if he'd paused to rest and never resumed moving.

"By the Light," Kaelen whispered, raising his hand. His palm began to glow with soft, holy radiance—the blessing he'd used a thousand times to grant peace to the dying, to ease suffering, to provide comfort.

"By the Light of the Order, I grant you—"

The moment his glow touched the old man, the frozen figure shrieked.

It wasn't a sound. It was a vibration—a soul-deep scream that bypassed Kaelen's ears entirely and resonated directly in his bones.

The old man didn't move, couldn't move, but the agony that poured from him was absolute.

Kaelen jerked back, his Light sputtering and dying. Through the tether, Elara felt his shock, his confusion, his dawning horror.

"Stop!" Elara grabbed his arm, pulling him away. "Your Light is burning them, Kaelen! To them, your 'holiness' feels like lye on an open wound. They aren't evil—they're just lingering. Your Light cannot help them. It's making it worse."

Kaelen stared at his hands—the hands that had dispensed the Order's justice for a decade, the hands that channeled the Light he'd been taught was the cure for all darkness. Those hands were weapons here. Instruments of torture.

"Then what do we do?" His voice was rough, stripped of certainty.

"We let me work," Elara said gently. She approached the young woman at the well, her movements slow and deliberate. She didn't use a decree or a prayer. She reached out, her fingers glowing with that soft, neon-pink light, and touched the woman's frozen shoulder.

As her magic made contact, Elara began to speak—not in the formal language of necromantic ritual, but in the warm, conversational tone of someone greeting an old friend.

"Hello, sweetheart," she murmured. "I know you're scared. I know you've been here a long time, stuck in this moment, unable to move forward or back. But I'm here now, and I'm going to help you remember. Remember the weight of the bucket when it's full of water. Remember the way your husband smiled when you brought it to him. Remember the feeling of the sun on your face before this place took the light away."

The pink glow intensified, flowing like liquid silk over the woman's frozen form. And slowly—so slowly—the rigidity began to ease. The woman's features relaxed, the tension bleeding out of her spectral presence. A soft sigh escaped her lips, her form beginning to dissolve into a flurry of pink petals that drifted away on a wind that shouldn't exist in this still place.

Peace. Not banishment. Not destruction. Peace.

One by one, Elara walked through the village. She didn't rush. She didn't force. She listened to their silences, helped them remember who they'd been, guided them home with the gentleness of a shepherd tending a flock.

Kaelen watched her work, and something fundamental shifted in his chest. This was the "vile witch" he'd been sent to guard. The practitioner of "foul arts" that the Order condemned. The woman who was supposed to represent everything wrong with the world.

And she was showing more mercy, more compassion, more genuine holiness than he'd seen in the Cathedral in years.

Hours passed. The moon rose—a pale, sickly thing barely visible through the canopy. Elara's glow grew dimmer with each spirit she released, her steps slower, her shoulders slumping under the weight of the work.

Finally, as the last spirit dissolved into peaceful nothingness, she collapsed against a stone wall, her chest heaving with exhaustion.

"They're all gone," she said, her voice barely a whisper. "Every single one. They're free now."

Kaelen approached slowly, his armor feeling heavier than ever. He looked at Elara—at the woman who had just spent hours doing what his entire Order couldn't do—and something in his carefully constructed worldview cracked like a pane of glass under a hammer.

"You did what I couldn't," he said quietly.

"I did what was necessary, Kaelen. There's a difference."

He looked down at his armor—the golden plate that represented his vows, his brothers, his god. The "Golden Lion" suit that had defined him for so long. It felt wrong now. Hollow. A costume he'd worn for a role he no longer understood.

His hand moved to the clasp at his throat—the golden fastening that held his cloak in place. The sun-sigil caught what little moonlight filtered through the trees, gleaming with that perfect, holy shine that represented everything the Order stood for.

Berenger had given it to him the day he'd taken his final vows. Kaelen could still remember the weight of his mentor's hand on his shoulder, the pride in those cold eyes.

"You've finally become the son I should have had," Berenger had said, pinning the clasp to Kaelen's cloak with hands that had scarred a twelve-year-old boy for hesitating. "Your father was weak. He put mercy above duty, and it destroyed him. But you—you've been purified by discipline. You understand what it means to serve without question, to execute justice without sentiment. This sigil marks you as mine. As the Order's. As perfection."

Kaelen had worn it every day since. Had polished it each morning alongside his armor. Had touched it before every battle, every arrest, every moment when he'd needed to remember what he was fighting for.

It had been a symbol of belonging. Of purpose. Of being chosen.

Now, standing in this village of trapped souls that his Light had tortured instead of saved, watching Elara collapse from the effort of doing what was actually holy, the sigil felt like a brand. Like a collar.

Like a lie he'd been telling himself for fifteen years.

He reached up and unbuckled the golden clasp, his fingers trembling slightly as they worked the mechanism. For a moment, he held it in his hands, feeling the weight of everything it represented. The weight of Berenger's approval. The weight of the Order's expectations. The weight of being "perfection" when perfection required closing your eyes to cruelty and calling it strength.

"You've been purified by discipline," Berenger had said.

But looking at Elara—exhausted, compassionate, kind despite the world's cruelty to her—Kaelen realized he'd been purified of the wrong things. Not of weakness or mercy or compassion. Those weren't impurities to be burned away.

Those were the parts of him that had made him human.

And Berenger had spent fifteen years teaching him to be ashamed of his humanity.

Kaelen let the sun-sigil fall.

It hit the dirt of the Silent Woods with a soft thud, the gold tarnishing instantly as it touched the corrupted soil. He stared at it for a long moment, then looked up at Elara.

"The Order told us the dead were an abomination," Kaelen whispered, not quite able to meet her eyes.

"The Order lies about a lot of things, darling," Elara said softly. She pushed herself up from the wall with visible effort and crossed to him, her hand reaching out to touch the dent in his chestplate—a mark from a battle weeks ago, before the tether, before he'd started to see her as anything other than a criminal.

"But you?" Her fingers traced the dented metal. "You're starting to see the truth."

Kaelen didn't pull away. Instead, he reached up and placed his hand over hers, holding it against the scarred metal over his heart. Through the tether, he felt her exhaustion, her sadness for the souls she'd freed, her quiet pride in him for finally seeing what she'd known all along.

"I don't know what I am anymore," he admitted, his voice rough. "The Order defined me. The Light was supposed to be absolute. Berenger taught me that certainty was strength, that questioning was weakness. But everything I was taught, everything I believed—it's all falling apart."

"Good," Elara said, and there was no mockery in her tone. Just gentle understanding. "Let it fall apart, Kaelen. You can't build something true on a foundation of lies. And the Order has been lying to you since you were ten years old."

He looked down at where their hands were joined—his scarred and calloused from years of swordwork, hers stained with dirt and glowing faintly with residual pink magic. Two people who should have been enemies. Were enemies, according to every law he'd sworn to uphold.

But the tether between them pulsed with something that felt suspiciously like trust. Like partnership.

Like the beginning of something neither of them had a name for yet.

"The sun-sigil," Elara said quietly, glancing at where it lay discarded in the dirt. "Berenger gave you that, didn't he?"

"The day I took my vows." Kaelen's jaw tightened. "He said I'd finally become the son he should have had. That I'd been purified."

"And you believed him."

"I wanted to believe him." The admission hurt. "I wanted to believe that all the pain, all the scars, all the times he'd hurt me—that it had all been for a purpose. That it had made me better. Stronger."

"It made you afraid," Elara said gently. "Afraid to hesitate. Afraid to show mercy. Afraid to be human. That's not strength, Kaelen. That's trauma disguised as training."

He couldn't argue with her. Not when the tether let her feel the truth of his emotions, the way his chest tightened at her words because she was right.

"I'm not him," Kaelen said finally, looking down at the discarded sigil. "I'm not going to be what Berenger made me. Not anymore."

"No," Elara agreed, her hand still pressed against his heart. "You're not."

Through the tether, he felt her certainty. Her absolute conviction that he was more than the Order's weapon, more than Berenger's "perfected" student.

He was Kaelen. Just Kaelen.

And maybe that was enough.

They stood like that for a long moment—her hand on his chest, his hand covering hers, the silver tether between them glowing softly in the darkness of the Silent Woods.

"We should rest," Elara said eventually, though she made no move to step away. "Tomorrow we reach the edge of the void-rift. And I have a feeling we're going to need all our strength."

"Elara," Kaelen said, his voice low. "Thank you."

"For what?"

"For showing me what holiness actually looks like."

She smiled—small and tired and genuine. "You're welcome, darling. Now help me find somewhere to sleep before I pass out in the dirt. I've maintained enough dignity for one day."

Kaelen helped her mount Cinder, leaving the sun-sigil where it had fallen. As they rode out of the Silent Woods—out of the village where Elara had freed hundreds of trapped souls while his Light had only caused pain—he didn't look back.

He wasn't a Paladin of the Light anymore.

He was something else. Something undefined. Something that terrified him and exhilarated him in equal measure.

And somehow, with Elara's arms around his waist and the tether pulsing steadily between them, that felt like exactly where he needed to be.

Chapter Nine

PINING & POLISHING

The transition from the Silent Woods to the outskirts of Blackpine Ridge felt like moving from a funeral to a fever dream.

The oppressive silence gave way to normal forest sounds—birds, insects, the rustle of small animals in the underbrush. But the silver tether between them was no longer just a humming nuisance; it was a live wire, transmitting every spike of Kaelen's residual adrenaline and every dip in Elara's dwindling energy.

They found a hollowed-out stone shed that had probably been used by charcoal burners before the void-rift had turned the region into a wasteland. It was cramped, smelled of damp earth and old soot, but it had a roof and four walls, which made it palatial compared to sleeping in the open.

Elara sat on a flat stone, her breathing shallow, her usual vibrant glow faded to the color of a bruised sunset. The work in the village had cost her more than she'd admitted. Her neon-pink magic had dimmed to barely a flicker, and a jagged graze from a stray void-shrike—incurred during their frantic exit from the woods when one of the corrupted birds had dive-bombed them—ran red and angry along her forearm.

She'd wrapped it hastily with a strip of her already-tattered lace, but blood was seeping through the makeshift bandage, and through the tether Kaelen could feel the sharp sting of pain she was trying to ignore.

"Sit still," he commanded, his voice rough with fatigue and something else—concern that he wasn't entirely comfortable acknowledging.

"I'm fine, Kaelen. I've had worse scratches from clumsy skeletons who don't know their own strength," Elara tried to joke, but the wit died in her throat as he knelt between her knees, his movements deliberate and careful despite the bulk of his armor.

He'd shed his gauntlets and pauldrons, leaving him in his sweat-stained gambeson. Without the full weight of the "Golden Lion" plate, he looked less like a statue of divine judgment and more like a man who was very, very tired of carrying the world on his shoulders.

"The Order's Light failed today," Kaelen said quietly, his voice barely audible over the crackle of the small fire he'd built. He produced a leather kit from his pack—sanctified salve, clean linen, a small vial of something that smelled of herbs and holy water. "It didn't just fail. It hurt them. I tried to help, and I caused pain."

He took her arm in his hands, his touch gentle despite the calluses. His skin was scorching hot against her cold, death-touched flesh—a reminder of the fundamental opposition between their magics.

"Kaelen—"

"I was taught that the Light is the only absolute," he interrupted, his blue eyes fixed on the wound as he carefully unwrapped the bloodied lace. "That everything the Order does is in service of a higher good. That doubt is weakness and questioning is corruption."

He dipped a cloth into the tin of salve. It should have stung—holy water was an ingredient, after all, blessed by priests and consecrated under the full moon—but Kaelen was murmuring a low, rhythmic prayer under his breath as he worked.

But this wasn't a prayer of banishment or judgment. It was a prayer of preservation. For the first time in his life, his Light wasn't being used as a weapon or a wall. It was being offered as a shield—gentle, protective, wrapping around her magic without trying to smother it.

The salve didn't burn. Instead, it cooled the wound, the holy properties and the death magic finding an unexpected harmony through the medium of Kaelen's genuine concern.

"Your magic was mercy today," Elara whispered, watching his face as he worked with the focused intensity of a man performing surgery. "What you did in that village—helping me calm the spirits, keeping watch so I could work, offering your strength when mine failed—that was holy, Kaelen. Not the armor. Not the decrees. You."

His hand stilled on her arm, his thumb tracing a slow, unconscious arc over the soft skin of her inner wrist, right where the silver tether emerged from her skin like a permanent bracelet.

Through the bond, Elara felt the war happening inside him. Years of conditioning screaming that this was wrong—that she was wrong, that necromancy was corruption, that any softness toward her was a failure of duty. But underneath that, stronger now, was the truth he'd witnessed with his own eyes.

She'd freed hundreds of souls today. With kindness. With compassion.

While his Light had only made them scream.

"You're staring," he muttered, but he didn't stop touching her. His thumb continued its slow, hypnotic path along her wrist, tracing the silver thread over and over.

"You have a smudge of soot on your cheek," she whispered, her usual bravado replaced by a terrifying vulnerability. "It's ruining the whole 'Saintly Warrior' aesthetic."

Kaelen didn't move to wipe it away. Instead, his eyes lifted to meet hers—and what she saw there made her breath catch.

Not just attraction. Not just the want that had been simmering between them since the moment they'd been tethered. This was something deeper. Something that looked suspiciously like reverence.

"The aesthetic died in the woods, Elara," he said, his voice low and rough. "I think I'd rather be a man than a saint."

The air in the shed became impossibly thick. The silver thread at their wrists pulsed—once, twice—sending a wave of pure, unadulterated longing through the connection. Not one-sided anymore. Both of them, wanting what they shouldn't want, knowing that crossing this line would change everything.

Kaelen's hand moved from her arm to the side of her neck, his calloused palm cupping her jaw with a tenderness that made her breath catch. His other hand remained on her bandaged forearm, thumb still tracing that maddening circle over her wrist.

"Kaelen," she breathed, half-warning, half-invitation.

"I know," he rasped, his forehead coming to rest against hers. His eyes closed, and for a moment he just breathed her in—graveyard dirt and peonies and something uniquely Elara that had haunted his dreams for three years.

Through the tether, she felt everything he was feeling. The desire, yes—hot and immediate and impossible to ignore. But also the fear. Fear that if he kissed her, if he crossed that final line, there would be no going back. Fear that he was betraying everything he'd ever been taught. Fear that this was the best thing that had ever happened to him and he didn't deserve it.

"I don't deserve this," he whispered against her skin, voicing the thought she'd felt through the bond. "Don't deserve you. I arrested you seventeen times, Elara. Seventeen times I dragged you away from your work, locked you in cells, treated you like a criminal—"

"Eighteen," she corrected softly, her hand coming up to cup his face, her thumb brushing over that smudge of soot. "You forgot the first arrest. Three years ago. I was twenty-two, you were freshly promoted to Golden Lion, and you were so certain I was evil."

"I was an idiot."

"You were doing what you'd been trained to do." Her fingers traced the sharp line of his jaw. "But you're not that person anymore. I can feel it through the tether. You're changing, Kaelen. Becoming who you were supposed to be before the Order got their hands on you."

"I don't know who that is," he admitted, the confession raw and painful.

"Then we'll figure it out together."

This was surrender. The "Golden Lion" hadn't just cracked; he had collapsed. The perfect paladin was dying, and in its place was just a man who'd realized that the person he'd been hunting, arresting, judging for years was the only thing in the world that felt real anymore.

"I'm going to ruin you," she whispered into the space between them, giving him one last chance to pull back, to remember his vows, to choose the safe path.

"Too late," he replied, his grip tightening just enough to let her know he wasn't letting go. "You already have."

He didn't kiss her—not yet. That line still felt too dangerous, too final. But he stayed there, forehead to forehead, breathing the same air, their hearts synchronized through the tether until Kaelen couldn't tell where his pulse ended and hers began.

The moment stretched, fragile and perfect. Outside, the wind picked up, rattling the shed's loose boards. Inside, the fire crackled, casting dancing shadows across the stone walls. And between them, the tether hummed with possibility.

Finally, with visible effort, Kaelen pulled back just enough to finish bandaging her wound. His hands were steady as he wrapped clean linen around her forearm, but through the tether she felt the storm raging inside him—duty warring with desire, loyalty to the Order battling against loyalty to the truth he'd seen today.

"There," he said quietly, securing the bandage with practiced efficiency. "That should hold until we can find proper supplies."

"Thank you," Elara said, and meant it for more than just the medical care.

When he was done, he didn't move away. Couldn't seem to, even though propriety and fifteen years of training screamed that he should put distance between them. Instead, he picked up a piece of silk— part of his travel kit, probably meant for polishing his armor—and began to clean his breastplate.

Not out of duty to the Order, but because he needed something to do with his hands before he did something he couldn't take back.

"You don't have to do that," Elara said, watching him work. "The armor, I mean. You left the sun-sigil behind. You could leave the rest of it too."

"I know." He rubbed at a particularly stubborn patch of dried blood. "But this armor... it's the only thing I've known for half my life. I'm not ready to completely shed it yet. Even if—" He stopped, swallowed hard. "Even if what it represents is dying."

"Then keep the armor," Elara said gently. "But make it mean something new. You're still a warrior, Kaelen. You're still strong, still protective, still willing to stand between people and the darkness. You don't need the Order's approval for that. You never did."

His hands stilled on the breastplate. Through the tether, she felt his gratitude, his grief, his tentative hope that maybe she was right.

The metal reflected the neon-pink glow of Elara's eyes in the firelight, and for the first time, the gold and the pink didn't clash.

They merged, creating something new.

Something that looked suspiciously like hope.

*   *   *

"We should sleep," Kaelen said eventually, though neither of them moved. "Tomorrow we push toward the rift itself. It's going to be worse than anything we've seen so far."

"I know." Elara shifted on her stone seat, wincing slightly as the movement pulled at her bandaged arm. "The earth has been getting sicker with every mile north. By tomorrow, there might not be any life left in the soil at all. Just... absence."

Kaelen finally set aside the polishing cloth and his armor. He spread out his bedroll—a simple affair of wool and canvas—and gestured for her to take it.

"I'm not taking your bed," Elara protested.

"We're sharing it," Kaelen said firmly. "The tether won't let us sleep more than fifty feet apart anyway, and I'm not spending another night on cold stone if I can help it. We'll split it. Like adults."

"You said that last time," Elara pointed out, but she was already moving toward the bedroll. "And we both know how well that worked out."

"This time there's no bolster to maintain the illusion of propriety," Kaelen said, a hint of dark humor in his voice. "So we'll just have to rely on self-control."

"And how's your self-control holding up?" Elara asked, settling onto the bedroll with a sigh of relief.

Through the tether, she felt his immediate, visceral response to having her lying on what was technically his bed, surrounded by his scent, close enough to touch.

"Poorly," he admitted, lying down beside her with careful precision, making sure there was at least a hand's width of space between them. "Very poorly."

They lay there in the firelight, not touching but achingly aware of each other. The tether pulsed between them, carrying every spike of want, every flutter of nervousness, every moment of wishing things were simpler.

"Kaelen?" Elara whispered into the darkness.

"Hmm?"

"What you said earlier. About being ruined." She turned her head to look at him. "I'm ruined too, you know. I've been alone for so long. Built walls so high I thought no one could ever get through. And then you—" Her voice caught. "Then you saw through all of it. Saw me. Not the necromancer. Not the criminal. Just... me."

Kaelen turned to face her, his blue eyes serious in the dim light. "You're not ruined, Elara. You're the strongest person I've ever met. And if I've gotten through your walls, it's only because you let me. Because under all that armor of sarcasm and sass, you wanted to be seen."

"Maybe I did," she admitted. "Maybe I've wanted someone to see me for a very long time."

His hand found hers in the space between them, fingers interlacing with the easy intimacy of people who'd been bound by more than just magic.

"I see you," he whispered. "And I'm terrified, and confused, and I don't know what I'm doing anymore. But I see you, Elara. And you're not a monster. You never were."

She squeezed his hand, feeling tears prick at the corners of her eyes. Through the tether, he felt them too—the overwhelm of being accepted, of being valued, of being seen as human after years of being treated as aberrant.

"Sleep," he said softly. "Tomorrow the rift. Tonight, just… rest."

"Stay with me?" The request slipped out before she could stop it, vulnerable and raw.

"Always," Kaelen promised, his thumb tracing circles over her knuckles. "Fifty feet or death, remember? You're stuck with me."

"I think I'm okay with that," Elara murmured, her eyes already drifting closed.

Through the tether, she felt his smile. Felt his contentment despite the fear and uncertainty. Felt him watching over her as she slipped into sleep, his hand still holding hers.

The Golden Lion was dying.

But Kaelen—just Kaelen—was learning how to live.

Chapter Ten

THE RUINS OF THE OLD KEEP

The ruins of Blackpine Keep didn't look like they had been destroyed by war. They looked like they had been consumed.

They'd reached the keep by mid-afternoon on the fifth day of travel—roughly eighty miles north of Oakhaven, twenty miles past the Silent Woods, and still another forty miles from the northern Oakhaven village that had gone completely silent. The keep sat at a strategic crossroads where the old trade routes converged before heading deeper into what was now the Grey Wastes. Before the void-rifts, this had been a military outpost, a watchtower guarding the northernmost reach of civilized territory.

Now it was a monument to erasure.

Stone that should have been weathered by centuries of wind and rain was instead pitted and porous, as if an invisible acid had been drizzling from the sky for years. The ivy climbing the walls wasn't green—it was a translucent, oily black that pulsed with a slow, sickly heartbeat that Elara could feel in her teeth.

The air itself was wrong. It tasted metallic, like blood and copper, and every breath made her magic recoil deeper into her chest as if trying to hide from something that wanted to devour it.

"I don't like it," Elara murmured, walking closer to Kaelen than the fifty-foot rule required—close enough that her shoulder brushed the edge of his dented pauldron with each step.

"The air is wrong," Kaelen agreed, his sword already drawn, the silver blade humming with residual power. He wasn't using his Holy Light to illuminate the path anymore—hadn't since the Silent Woods. Instead, he relied on the neon-pink glow emanating from Elara's fingertips.

It was a quiet admission. A small surrender. An acknowledgment that his god was no longer welcome on this journey, but she was.

"It's not just wrong, Kaelen. It's hungry." Elara stopped in front of the Great Hall's arched entrance, her magic flaring brighter as she tested the darkness beyond. "The spirits here aren't lingering. They've been erased. There's a hollow space where the history of this place should be. It's like someone took a knife and cut out every memory, every death, every piece of the past."

They stepped inside, boots crunching on debris. The ceiling had collapsed in places, allowing the bruised purple sky of the borderlands to peek through the rafters. Dust motes hung in the air, suspended as if gravity had given up halfway.

In the center of the hall stood a massive stone dais. It should have held a throne, or a statue of whatever lord had ruled here. Instead, it held a rift.

The void-rift was small—no larger than a man's head—but it radiated wrongness like a wound radiates fever.

It wasn't black. Black was a color, something that existed in the spectrum of light. This was the absolute absence of color, of light, of existence itself. The edges of the tear didn't sit cleanly in three-dimensional space—they fractured outward in impossible geometries, creating visual echoes that hurt to track with the eye. Looking at it was like trying to focus on a reflection in shattered glass, except the glass was reality itself and the shards were cutting through multiple dimensions simultaneously.

The rift had depth that shouldn't exist. Elara could see layers behind layers—not distance, but recursion. The darkness folded back on itself infinitely, each fold containing another void, creating a dizzying sense of falling inward while standing perfectly still.

Around the tear's perimeter, space itself was... uncertain. Objects near the rift appeared to flicker between states of existence—solid, then translucent, then inverted as if reality couldn't decide whether they were real or not. A fallen stone near the base of the dais seemed to occupy multiple positions at once, blurred at the edges like a long-exposure photograph of something moving too fast to capture.

The air around the rift didn't just shimmer—it tore. Elara could see microscopic fractures spreading outward from the central void, hairline cracks in the fabric of existence that caught what little light remained and refracted it into colors that shouldn't exist: not-quite-ultraviolet, beyond-infrared, shades that her eyes registered as painful static.

And through it all, there was movement. Not in the rift, but of the rift itself. It pulsed with a slow, rhythmic breathing, expanding and contracting like a living wound trying to tear itself wider. With each pulse, the fractal edges spread a little further, the reality-distortion radius grew by another inch, and the space around it became a little less certain about what "space" even meant.

"The void-rift," Kaelen breathed, stepping toward it despite every instinct screaming at him to run.

"Don't get too close," Elara warned, her hand flying to the silver tether at her wrist. "If that thing touches your soul, it won't just kill you. It will unmake you. You'll become one of those Hollowed things we saw in the woods—a body without a spirit, a puppet with its strings cut."

Kaelen ignored the warning, his eyes fixed on something at the base of the dais. He knelt, his armored knee cracking against stone, and brushed away a thick layer of grey soot.

"Elara. Look at this."

She leaned over his shoulder, following his gaze. Carved into the stone, surrounding the rift in a perfect, geometric circle, were a series of runes. They weren't the chaotic, jagged symbols she'd expect from something born of the Void. They were precise. Elegant. Mathematical in their perfection.

They were the High Order's liturgical script.

"Those are binding sigils," Elara said slowly, her voice losing all its playful edge. She knelt beside him, tracing one of the symbols with a trembling finger, careful not to actually touch the stone. "But they're inverted. These aren't meant to keep the Void out, Kaelen. They're meant to pull it through. To anchor it here. To keep it stable and feeding."

"No," Kaelen rasped, but the word came out hollow, unconvincing even to his own ears. "The High Priest said the Rifts were a divine punishment. A natural disaster caused by 'heretical magic' like yours. He said—"

"Does this look natural to you?" Elara gestured to the center of the circle, her hand shaking with rage. Nestled in a small groove in the stone, protected by a glass case that had somehow survived the collapse around it, was a fragment of a silver mirror. The same kind of mirror the Paladins used to focus their Holy Light. The same kind that hung in every Cathedral, in every shrine, in every holy place across the realm.

It was a conductor. A lens. A tool.

"They're using the Light to anchor the Shadow," Elara said, her voice deadly quiet. "They aren't fighting the Void, Kaelen. They're farming it. Creating it. Controlling it. And then riding in as saviors to 'protect' people from the very thing they unleashed."

Kaelen stood abruptly, his armor clashing with a sound that echoed through the dead hall. He looked at his reflection in his polished breastplate—the Lion of the Order, golden and perfect and utterly, irredeemably built on lies.

Everything he had ever done—every "heretic" he had arrested, every vow he had taken, every time he'd looked at Elara and seen corruption instead of mercy—had been in service to a monstrous deception.

The "monsters" he had been told to hunt were symptoms of a plague his own masters were spreading.

"They're using the Rifts to clear the borderlands," he realized, his voice cold with a fury so deep it felt like ice in his veins. "Territorial expansion under the guise of a holy crusade. They destroy the villages, blame the 'darkness,' and then move in to 'purify' the land for the Order. They get more territory, more control, more power. And anyone who questions it is labeled a heretic."

Elara watched him process the betrayal, and her heart ached for the man whose entire identity was shattering in real-time. She reached out, her hand hesitating before settling on the center of his chest, right over his heart.

"Kaelen," she said softly. "I'm sorry."

He looked down at her, his eyes hard and bright with unshed tears. "You're sorry? Elara, they were going to execute you for 'causing' the very thing they built. They've killed thousands—tens of thousands—and blamed people like you."

"I knew they were bastards, Kaelen," she said, trying to smile but failing. "I just didn't know they were this efficient at being bastards."

A sound outside the hall made them both freeze.

Hoofbeats. Fast, desperate, getting closer.

Kaelen's hand went to his sword hilt immediately, and Elara's magic flared pink as they moved as one toward the entrance. Through the tether, she felt his combat readiness, his protective instinct flaring hot and immediate.

A rider burst through the ruined gates of the keep, his horse lathered and wild-eyed. The man was young—maybe twenty—wearing the brown leather of a messenger, not the white and gold of the Order. His face was pale, streaked with dirt and what might have been tears.

He pulled his horse to a sliding stop when he saw them, his eyes going wide at the sight of Kaelen's golden armor.

"Paladin!" the messenger gasped, half-falling from his saddle. "Thank the Light—I've been riding for three days trying to find help. The northern village—Oakhaven-North—it's—" He stopped, swallowing hard. "Everyone's gone. Not dead. Just... gone. Turned into those frozen things, those Hollowed. And it's spreading. The rift is growing, and—"

"We know," Kaelen said, his voice grim. "We're heading there now. How far ahead are we?"

"Two days' hard ride," the messenger said. "Maybe less if you don't stop. But sir, you can't—the rift there, it's huge. Ten times the size of anything I've ever heard of. The entire village is just... swallowed by it. And the Order—" He stopped, seeming to realize he was speaking to a Paladin. "The Order says it's divine judgment. Says the village harbored heretics and this is their punishment."

"The Order is lying," Kaelen said flatly, and the messenger's eyes went even wider. "What's your name?"

"Jaxon, sir. I'm—I was—a courier for the trade routes. But there are no trade routes anymore. Just... emptiness."

Kaelen studied the young man's face, something nagging at him. There was a familiarity there—in the sharp line of the jaw, the cold grey eyes that seemed to calculate everything. Eyes he'd seen before, in the High Priest's chambers.

"Jaxon," Kaelen said carefully. "Your family name?"

The messenger hesitated, and in that hesitation, Kaelen saw years of practiced evasion. "My mother never used one. She said names only mattered to people who wanted to be remembered by history. We were just... border folk."

It was a deflection, and they both knew it. But Kaelen didn't press.

"Do you have family in the north?" he asked instead.

The messenger's face crumpled. "Had. My mother. My sister. They lived in Oakhaven-North. When the rift came, they..." He couldn't finish. "My mother always said the Light would protect us if we were faithful. She believed that until the end. Even when the Cathedral sent no help. Even when they called it 'divine judgment.'"

There was something raw and bitter in those words, something that spoke of a deeper betrayal than just abandoned villages.

Elara stepped forward, her pink magic dimming to something gentler. Through the tether, she felt Kaelen's grief for this young man, his fury at the Order that had destroyed Jaxon's family and then called it holy.

"We're going to stop this," Elara said quietly. "I promise you. We're going to close the rift, and we're going to make sure the people responsible answer for what they've done."

Jaxon looked at her—really looked at her—and seemed to notice the pink glow, the tether connecting her to the Paladin, the fact that she was clearly a practitioner of death magic standing beside a Golden Lion.

"You're a necromancer," he said, but there was no accusation in his voice. Just exhaustion. "They said necromancers caused this."

"They lied about that too," Kaelen said. "She's trying to fix it. We both are."

Jaxon studied them for a long moment, then nodded slowly. "Then I'm coming with you. I know the paths north better than anyone. I can get you there faster, and..." His voice hardened. "I want to see it. I want to see what they did. And I want them to pay."

Kaelen and Elara exchanged a glance through the tether. They both knew bringing a civilian into a void-rift was dangerous. But they also knew that Jaxon deserved to know the truth. Deserved to be part of stopping it.

"Can you fight?" Kaelen asked.

"I can learn," Jaxon said. "Please. Don't make me go back to Oakhaven and just... wait. I need to do something. Anything."

Kaelen looked at Elara, and she nodded slightly. Through the bond, he felt her compassion, her understanding. She'd been where Jaxon was—powerless, dismissed, told to stay quiet while the powerful made decisions.

"You'll follow orders," Kaelen said firmly. "You'll stay back when we tell you to stay back. And if things get bad—"

"I know the risks," Jaxon interrupted. "I've seen what those rifts do. I'm not going in blind."

"Then welcome to the rebellion," Elara said with a small, grim smile. "We're overthrowing corrupt gods and exposing institutional evil. It's very trendy right now."

Jaxon managed a weak laugh, and some of the haunted look left his eyes.

"Rest your horse," Kaelen commanded, already moving back toward the dais. "We need to destroy this rift first, then we head north. Elara, can you—"

"Already on it," she said, her magic flaring as she approached the inverted binding sigils.

Kaelen reached down and picked up the silver mirror fragment with his bare hand, not bothering with gloves or protection. He held it up to the dim light, watching the way it refracted and bent the shadows.

Then he closed his fist around it and crushed it.

The mirror screamed—a high, keening sound like reality itself protesting—and shattered into dust that sparkled as it fell through his fingers.

The void-rift pulsed once, violently, then began to collapse in on itself. The fractal edges pulled inward, the spatial distortions smoothing, reality knitting itself back together with visible relief. Within seconds, the rift was gone, leaving only a scorched circle on the stone where it had been anchored.

"We aren't just going to the border to close a rift," Kaelen said, his voice dropping into a register that made the silver tether hum with dangerous, dark energy. "We're going back to Oakhaven. And I'm going to burn that Cathedral to the ground. I'm going to drag the High Priest into the light of day, and I'm going to make sure every single person in that city knows exactly what he's done."

Elara felt a thrill of terror and something else—something that felt suspiciously like pride. Her Paladin hadn't just fallen from grace. He had decided to take the whole corrupt edifice down with him.

"Well," Elara whispered, her neon-pink glow flaring to a brilliant, defiant fuchsia. "I did say I'd be a bad influence on you, Sir Kaelen. I just didn't think you'd be such a fast learner."

The silver tether between them glowed—no longer a chain of restraint, but a fused, incandescent declaration of war.

The logistics of their souls had changed forever.

They weren't warden and prisoner anymore.

They were two halves of the same rebellion.

And now they had their first recruit.

Chapter Eleven

THE RAINSTORM

The sky didn't just break; it shattered.

The storm came on with the violence of divine retribution, as if the world itself was weeping for the truth they'd uncovered. It wasn't a cleansing rain—it was a deluge of iron-grey water that smelled of old pennies and wet stone, the kind of storm that felt like nature trying to wash away the memory of what had been done to Blackpine Keep.

They'd left Jaxon to return to Oakhaven with news of what they'd found—someone had to warn the city, and the young courier knew the southern routes better than anyone. He'd promised to gather allies, to spread word of the Order's corruption to anyone who would listen. It was dangerous work, but Jaxon had insisted, his grief over his family transforming into purpose.

Now it was just Elara and Kaelen again, pushing north through increasingly hostile territory.

"In there!" Kaelen shouted over the roar of wind and water, pointing his sword toward a jagged opening in a limestone cliff.

He didn't wait for Elara's response. He grabbed Cinder's bridle with one hand and Elara's waist with the other, hauling both toward the narrow cave entrance. They scrambled inside, the silver tether between them jerking and sparking as it scraped against wet stone.

Inside, the cave was mercifully dry, smelling of ancient dust and the faint, sweet scent of Elara's peony-tinted magic. Kaelen led Cinder to the back, his breath coming in ragged white plumes that spoke of exertion and adrenaline and the crushing weight of what he'd learned at the Keep.

"I'm soaked," Elara gasped, her teeth chattering so hard she could barely speak. Her dark hair was plastered to her forehead, the neon-pink streaks glowing faintly against the wet brown like veins of living light, her lace sleeves heavy with rain and mud. "My boots are serving as personal aquariums. If I find a fish in here, Kaelen, I'm holding you personally responsible for the state of the weather."

Kaelen didn't answer. He was moving with frantic, mechanical efficiency—unsaddling Cinder, his hands shaking not from cold but from the aftershocks of rage that he was barely containing. He piled the leather gear in a corner and turned toward Elara, and she saw it in his eyes.

He was breaking.

Not just his faith. Him. The foundation of everything he'd built his identity on was crumbling, and he was desperately trying not to collapse with it.

"Get your cloak off," he said, his voice rough and strained. "We need a fire, or the damp will settle in your lungs and—"

"Kaelen." Elara's voice was gentle, cutting through his spiral. "Breathe."

"I'm fine."

"You're not fine." She started unlacing her soaked outer layer, peeling off the wet fabric with movements slowed by cold and exhaustion. "You just found out your entire life has been a lie. You're allowed to not be fine."

Kaelen reached into his pack and pulled out a bundle of dry tinder wrapped in oilcloth—the preparation of a man who never expected the world to be kind. With a few strikes of flint, a small orange flame flickered to life, and he built it carefully into something that could actually provide warmth.

Elara huddled near the fire, her knees pulled to her chest, watching him. The orange light clashed with the neon-pink of her skin, creating a strange violet aura that made her look otherworldly. She could see the tension in every line of his body—the way his shoulders were locked tight, the way his jaw clenched and unclenched as he tried to process what they'd discovered.

He stood by the cave's mouth, staring out at the wall of rain, his hands gripping the stone so tightly his knuckles had gone white.

"Kaelen," she said softly. "The armor. Take it off."

He stiffened. "I'm fine."

"You're vibrating. And not in the fun, 'magic-tether' way. You're freezing, and that metal is holding the cold against your skin like a tomb. It's the middle of a storm, we're alone in a cave, and there isn't a single person for miles who cares about the Order's rules." She crawled closer, her eyes catching his. "Take. It. Off. Or I'll have Arthur come back and haunt your peripheral vision for a month with explicit commentary on your poor life choices."

Kaelen let out a long, shuddering breath that might have been a laugh or might have been a sob. Slowly—so slowly—he reached for the buckles of his breastplate.

In the quiet of the cave, the sound of the metal hitting the stone floor was deafening. One by one, the pieces fell: the pauldrons, the bracers, the greaves. Finally, he sat down across from her in nothing but his damp linen tunic and trousers, and without the gold he looked smaller.

More human.

Utterly, devastatingly broken.

"They call me the Golden Lion," he whispered, his eyes fixed on the fire. His voice was hollow, scraped raw. "Do you know why?"

"Because you have a very expensive tailor and questionable taste in nicknames?" Elara offered, but her voice lacked its usual bite.

"Because I was the perfect vessel," Kaelen said, ignoring her attempt at levity. "I didn't question. I didn't feel. I didn't doubt. I was the purest blade the High Priest had—sharp, obedient, and completely unaware that I was being used to carve his empire out of innocent flesh."

He looked at his hands—scarred, callused, stained with the blood of people who had probably done nothing wrong except be in the way of the Order's expansion.

"I spent years perfecting that persona," he continued, his voice breaking. "I made myself into a statue so I wouldn't have to look at what I was actually doing. I thought if I was shiny enough, faithful enough, golden enough, then it would all mean something. That the sacrifices would be worth it. That I was serving a higher purpose."

He looked up at her, and the vulnerability in his gaze made her breath catch.

"I hate him, Elara."

"The High Priest?"

"No," Kaelen rasped, and now the tears were falling, carving tracks through the grime on his face. "The Lion. I hate the man they made me be. I hate the way people look at the armor and see a savior when all I've ever been is a well-dressed executioner. I hate that I believed them. That I hurt people because someone told me it was holy."

The silence that followed was filled only by the drumming of rain and the crackle of fire. Elara reached out, her fingers hovering over the silver tether before settling on Kaelen's knee—a small touch, but permission to be human.

"You aren't the armor, Kaelen," she said, her voice steady despite the tears threatening in her own eyes. "The Lion is what they built. But the man who cleaned my wound in the shed? The man who dropped his cloak in the Silent Woods because he couldn't stomach the lie anymore? The man who just crushed that mirror because he'd rather burn the world down than serve a corrupt god? That's who you are."

"A traitor," he said bitterly.

"A rebel," she corrected, her hand sliding from his knee to his hand, threading their fingers together. "And for the record? I like the rebel much better. He's much more interesting. Better at brooding, too."

Kaelen's lips twitched—not quite a smile, but close. He squeezed her hand, his thumb tracing the line of the silver tether where it emerged from her skin.

"Why are you still here, Elara?" he asked, his voice raw with genuine confusion. "You could have run a dozen times. The tether is strong enough now that you could probably stretch it, find a way to break it. You're powerful enough. So why stay with a broken paladin who's going to get you killed?"

Elara looked down at their joined hands—her small, pale fingers wrapped in his large, scarred ones. Through the tether, she could feel everything he was feeling: the grief, the rage, the bone-deep exhaustion, and underneath it all, a fierce, desperate love that he was too afraid to name.

"Because, Sir Kaelen," she whispered, meeting his eyes, "I think I'm the only one who knows where the real you has been hiding all these years. And I've always had a thing for lost causes." She paused, her neon-pink eyes glowing in the firelight. "Also, you give excellent existential crisis. Very compelling. Ten out of ten, would witness emotional breakdown again."

That did it. Kaelen laughed—a real, genuine laugh that sounded rusty from disuse but beautiful nonetheless. He pulled her close, wrapping his arms around her, burying his face in her rain-soaked hair.

"I'm not a hero," he warned, his voice muffled against her neck.

"Good," she breathed, her arms wrapping around his waist, holding him together while he fell apart. "I've had enough of heroes. Give me the man instead."

They stayed like that for a long moment, wrapped in each other, the warmth of their bodies cutting through the damp chill of the cave. Through the tether, emotions flowed freely—his grief, her acceptance, his fear, her certainty, his love that he still couldn't voice, her love that she'd known about for far too long.

"Tomorrow," Kaelen said finally, his voice steadier now, "we reach the northern village. We see what the main rift looks like. And then—"

"And then we go back to Oakhaven," Elara finished. "And we burn it all down."

"Metaphorically," Kaelen clarified, though there was a dark amusement in his voice. "Mostly metaphorically."

"Mostly," Elara agreed, grinning against his chest.

The rain continued to howl outside, but inside the cave, surrounded by the warmth of the fire and the steady pulse of the soul-tether, two broken people held each other and pretended—just for tonight—that falling in love during the apocalypse wasn't the worst possible timing.

Tomorrow, they would plan a revolution.

Tonight, they would simply survive each other.

Chapter Twelve

THE TRAITOR REVEALED

The morning after the storm didn't bring clarity; it brought a thick, claustrophobic mist that clung to the valley floor like the ghosts Elara usually commanded.

Kaelen was back in his armor—he'd had no choice, really, given that it was the only protection he had—but the fit was different now. The metal didn't feel like a second skin anymore; it felt like a cage. A costume for a role he no longer believed in. He hadn't polished it. The dents from the Keep remained, dull and accusing in the grey light.

Beside him, Elara was uncharacteristically quiet, her fingers tracing the silver tether with a restless, rhythmic motion that told him she was thinking. Planning. Worrying about something she hadn't voiced yet.

"Someone's coming," Kaelen said, his voice dropping into that low, tactical register that usually preceded violence. His hand went instinctively to his sword hilt.

He didn't need to point. Through the shifting veil of fog, the rhythmic clip-clop of a disciplined gallop echoed against the canyon walls. This wasn't a traveler or a merchant. This was a rider on a mission, moving with military precision.

"Hide," Kaelen commanded, his hand on Elara's shoulder as he guided her toward a cluster of weeping willow trees whose grey-green branches hung like curtains.

"Kaelen, I'm a necromancer, not a housecat," Elara hissed, though she stayed behind the natural cover. "I don't 'hide.'"

"You do when I say so," he snapped, but through the tether she felt his fear—not of the rider, but for her. "If it's a Purifier, they'll kill you before you can even finish one of your snappy comebacks. Please, Elara. Just this once, let me handle it."

The unspoken "I can't lose you" hung in the air between them, transmitted through the bond more clearly than words ever could.

Elara nodded, pressing herself against the tree trunk, and watched as Kaelen stepped into the center of the road. He didn't draw his sword. He stood like the statue he hated—the Golden Lion, perfect and untouchable, waiting.

The rider broke through the mist like an arrow. He wore the white-and-gold surcoat of the Sun-Sparrows—the High Order's elite messengers, chosen for their speed and their absolute loyalty. When he saw Kaelen, he pulled back on the reins so hard his stallion neighed in protest.

"Sir Kaelen!" the messenger gasped, sliding off his horse with the graceless haste of someone who'd been riding too hard for too long. He was young—barely twenty, with the kind of earnest face that hadn't yet learned to hide fear or doubt. "Praise the Sun. We thought you were lost in the Keep's collapse."

Kaelen recognized him. Torin. One of the newer recruits, barely out of his training robes, assigned to messenger duty because he was fast and eager and hadn't yet learned that eagerness could get you killed.

"Torin," Kaelen said carefully, his eyes scanning the young man for weapons, for signs of hostility, for anything that might indicate this was a trap. "What are you doing this far from the Capital?"

Torin reached into his tunic and pulled out a scroll sealed with the High Priest's personal signet—a sun rising over a mountain of skulls, rendered in red wax that looked disturbingly like dried blood.

"I have urgent missives for the Border Commander," Torin said, his voice shaking slightly. "But since you're here, you need to see the update to the Cleansing Protocol. The High Priest said the Light-Blight is spreading faster than anticipated. We're to accelerate the evacuations and—"

Kaelen's hand shot out, grabbing Torin's wrist before the young man could finish. Through the contact, Kaelen felt it—a faint, vibrating hum. The same frequency as the void-rift at Blackpine Keep.

"Where did you get this scroll, Torin?" Kaelen asked, his voice deathly quiet.

"The Cathedral's inner sanctum, sir. The High Priest handed it to me personally. He said it was critical that—"

"When did you start feeling cold?" Kaelen interrupted, his eyes dropping to where his hand gripped Torin's wrist.

The young messenger blinked, confused. "I... what?"

"Your hands, Torin. When did they start going cold? When did you start having trouble sleeping? When did the nightmares begin?"

Torin's face went pale. "How did you... I thought it was just the stress of the mission. The High Priest said it was a test of faith, that if I remained pure the symptoms would—"

"Look at your hands," Kaelen commanded, releasing his grip.

Torin looked down, and Elara—watching from the trees—saw the exact moment the young man's world shattered. Faint purple veins were crawling up his wrists from the very scroll he carried, spreading like ink through water, pulsing with that same sickly rhythm.

"What... what is this?" Torin's voice pitched high with panic.

From her hiding place, Elara stepped out, unable to watch the young man's terror without offering help. The silver tether pulled taut as she moved, and Torin's eyes went wide when he saw her—saw the connection between the legendary Golden Lion and a dark-haired necromancer whose scattered pink streaks marked her as something other than ordinary.

"The Light you're carrying isn't pure, Torin," Elara said gently, her magic flaring as she examined him from a distance. "It's contaminated. Weaponized. They're using you as a delivery system for Void corruption. Every person you've given messages to, every commander you've briefed—you've been spreading the very thing the Order claims to fight."

Through the tether, Kaelen felt Elara's rage on Torin's behalf—this boy was a victim, just another tool the Order had used and discarded.

"I... I didn't know," Torin whispered, dropping the scroll as if it had burned him. "I was told I was a hero. That I was serving the Light. That my missions were saving lives."

"That's how they get you," Kaelen said, his voice thick with a bitterness born of recognition. He saw himself in this boy—the eagerness, the faith, the absolute certainty that the Order was righteous. "They make you believe that service is salvation. That obedience is holiness. That questioning is weakness."

He looked at Elara, then back at Torin. The choice was clear: tell the boy the truth and make him a target, or let him continue in ignorance and become a weapon.

Kaelen had spent his entire life choosing duty over truth.

Not anymore.

"Torin," he said, picking up the fallen scroll. "I need you to listen very carefully. The High Order is not what you think it is. The void-rifts—they're not a natural plague. They're weapons. Created by the Order. By the High Priest himself."

He broke the seal and unrolled the parchment. His eyes scanned the contents, and through the tether Elara felt his heart stop.

It wasn't just words. There were diagrams. Technical specifications. The scroll detailed "Operation Solar Flare"—a protocol for using concentrated Holy Light to create controlled void-rifts in specific locations. Target maps showed the border provinces marked for "neutralization." Population estimates were listed beside each village, with notations about "acceptable losses" and "territorial acquisition timelines."

This wasn't a defense plan. It was a blueprint for genocide dressed up as salvation.

"The total neutralization of the border provinces," Elara read over his shoulder, her voice shaking with fury, "to ensure 'uncontested ecclesiastical sovereignty.' They're not saving people, Torin. They're clearing the land so the Order can claim it. The Void is their vacuum cleaner, and you're part of the mechanism."

Torin looked between them—at the legendary Golden Lion who had just called the High Priest a liar, at the necromancer who was supposed to be his enemy but was looking at him with genuine compassion.

"I've been carrying these orders for six months," Torin said, his voice breaking. "I've delivered messages to twelve different commanders. I've touched… gods, I've touched hundreds of people. Have I been poisoning them all?"

"Not directly," Elara said. "The contamination is slow. Designed to spread over time. But yes—you've been a vector. Not by choice. Not knowingly. But the result is the same."

A high-pitched, metallic whistle pierced the mist—a signal flare, the kind the Purifiers used to coordinate ambushes.

Torin's face went white. "They followed me," he whispered, terror draining the last color from his cheeks. "The Purifiers. They said if I didn't return within the hour with confirmation of delivery, they'd 'sanitize' my route. I thought they meant bandits. I thought—"

"They meant witnesses," Kaelen said flatly. He looked at Elara, and through the tether she felt his tactical mind already running scenarios, calculating odds, preparing for battle. "They sent him as bait. To see if I was still loyal. To see if I'd question the orders."

The silver tether between them was white-hot now, vibrating with a warning that made the hair on Kaelen's arms stand up. The Purifiers were close. Very close.

"Torin," Kaelen said, his command voice snapping back into place. "Take your horse and ride south. Don't go back to the Order. Head for the neutral territories. Find work as a courier somewhere they don't ask questions. Change your name if you have to. But do not return to Oakhaven."

"And you, sir?"

Kaelen looked at the silver tether, then at Elara. He reached up and slowly, deliberately, began to unbuckle the heavy sun-sigil from his chest—the primary symbol of his rank, the mark that identified him as a Paladin of the Light.

He threw it into the mud at his feet.

"I'm staying with the heretic," Kaelen said, his gaze locking onto Elara's. Through the bond, she felt his absolute certainty, his fierce protectiveness, his willingness to burn the entire world down if it meant keeping her safe.

Torin stared at the discarded symbol, at the Golden Lion choosing a necromancer over the sun itself, and something in his young face hardened with understanding.

"The Order lied to us," Torin said. Not a question. A statement.

"Yes," Kaelen confirmed.

"All of it? Everything we were taught?"

"Not everything," Elara said gently. "Light exists. So does darkness. But the men claiming to speak for the Light? They're just men. Fallible. Corrupt. Human. And they've been using your faith as a weapon."

Torin nodded once, sharp and final. He mounted his horse, but before he could ride away, he looked back at Kaelen.

"Thank you, sir. For telling me the truth."

"Thank me by surviving," Kaelen replied. "And by remembering that faith in an ideal is not the same as loyalty to the institution that claims to represent it."

Torin rode off into the mist, and within seconds he was gone—swallowed by the grey.

Kaelen turned to Elara. The sound of approaching horses was growing louder. Multiple riders. Heavy armor. The distinctive hum of blessed weapons being drawn and charged.

The Purifiers were coming.

"Elara," Kaelen said, his hand going to his sword, "if we die today, I want you to know something."

"Don't," she said, stepping close to him, her hand finding his. "Don't you dare give me a goodbye speech, Kaelen. We're not dying today."

"How can you be so sure?"

Elara's grin was sharp and bright and absolutely feral. "Because I've already got a few dozen ghosts on standby. And they're dying—well, re-dying—to meet your brothers."

The mist ahead of them began to glow with sickly, artificial gold. The Purifiers had found them.

The hunt was officially on.

Chapter Thirteen

THE AMBUSH

The mist didn't just part; it was incinerated.

A wall of artificial, blindingly white light tore through the grey fog like a knife through cloth, smelling of ozone and burning incense and the particular brand of righteousness that came from men who had never once questioned their orders.

Kaelen shoved Elara behind a moss-covered boulder, his body moving on pure combat instinct. His hand was already on his hilt, gripping the leather so hard it groaned.

"Stay low," he commanded, his voice dropping into that battlefield register that expected immediate obedience. "The Purifiers don't aim for the heart. They aim to 'sanitize' the area. That means everything within twenty yards becomes acceptable collateral damage."

"How very thorough of them," Elara whispered, though her usual snark was thinned by the sight of what emerged from the burning mist.

Six figures in full blessed plate, their armor polished to a mirror sheen that was designed to reflect Holy Light back at their enemies until they were blinded and disoriented. They moved in perfect synchronization—the kind of coordination that came from years of training together, fighting together, killing together.

Leading them was a man Kaelen recognized by the way he held his longsword—blade angled slightly down and to the left, a defensive stance that could shift to offense in a heartbeat.

Sir Berenger. The man who had taught Kaelen how to parry before he'd even grown tall enough to reach the training dummy's chest. The man who had stood beside him through a dozen campaigns, who had been more of a father to him than his actual father ever was.

The man who was now here to kill him.

"Sir Kaelen," Berenger's voice was a deep, resonant boom that carried across the clearing despite the mist. It was the voice Kaelen had once associated with safety, with guidance, with the absolute certainty that someone older and wiser knew the right path. "Step away from the abomination. The High Priest is merciful. He says your soul can still be scrubbed clean if you deliver the girl to us now. This doesn't have to end in bloodshed."

Kaelen stepped out from behind the boulder, and Elara's heart clenched as she watched him deliberately position himself between her and the six armored killers. He didn't have his sun-sigil anymore—had thrown it away just minutes ago—but his scarred breastplate and dull armor still marked him as one of them.

Or at least, as what he used to be.

"The only thing that needs scrubbing, Berenger," Kaelen said, his voice steady and cold, "is the Cathedral floor. I've seen the mirrors. I've seen the Operation Solar Flare protocol. You aren't purging the darkness—you're planting it. You're murdering innocents and calling it holy work."

A ripple of movement went through the Purifiers—surprise, confusion, the first seeds of doubt. But Berenger's stance didn't shift. If anything, he seemed almost... sad.

"Heresy is a symptom of the rot, Kaelen," Berenger said, his voice taking on the tone of a teacher explaining a difficult lesson to a slow student. "You've been tethered to a parasite for too long. The death magic has clouded your mind, corrupted your thoughts. It's twisted your perception until you cannot see the Light anymore."

"I can see it just fine, Berenger," Kaelen replied. "I can see that it's being used to create the very darkness we're supposed to fight. I can see that every Rift, every 'corrupted' village, every 'necessary purge' has been manufactured by the Order to justify expansion. How many innocent people have we killed in the name of your perfect Light?"

"They weren't innocent!" Berenger's control cracked for just a moment, his sword hand tightening on the grip. "They were obstacles. Hindrances to the greater good. The Order provides structure, provides purpose, provides salvation to a world that would collapse into chaos without us. Individual lives are meaningless measured against the eternal peace we're building."

"You actually believe that," Kaelen said, and through the tether Elara felt his grief, his disbelief that the man who had been his mentor could have fallen so far into the lie. "You believe the words, don't you? You're not lying. You genuinely think that murder in the service of order is holier than mercy in the service of truth."

"Silence, witch!" Berenger barked, his attention snapping to where Elara had emerged from behind the boulder to stand beside Kaelen. "By the Light of the Unconquered Sun, I sentence you both to purification by Flame. May your souls be cleansed of the rot."

The Purifiers moved as one, forming a perfect V-formation, their armor beginning to glow with searing, concentrated heat. This wasn't the gentle warmth of Kaelen's protective Light. This was Sun-Fire— the Order's executioner's tool, designed to burn away corruption so thoroughly that not even ash remained.

"Elara, now!" Kaelen roared, and he didn't draw on the Sun. He couldn't—not anymore, not after everything he'd learned. Instead, he drew on the only thing he had left that felt real.

The silver tether.

He reached out with his mind, grabbing the connection between him and Elara, and pulled. The thread between them didn't just glow—it became a conduit, a bridge, a channel through which their combined power could flow.

Elara slammed her palms onto the earth, her magic erupting in a violent cascade of neon-pink that lit up the mist like a second sun.

"Arthur! Marcus! Every grumpy ancestor in a three-mile radius who died angry at the establishment—GET UP!"

The ground beneath the Purifiers' feet didn't shake; it exploded.

Skeletons clad in the rotted leather of long-dead woodcutters and ancient border guards clawed their way out of the dirt with the fury of people who had been silenced for too long. But these weren't the slow, stumbling zombies of children's nightmares. Infused with Elara's neon-pink spite and Kaelen's raw, defensive energy channeled through the soul-tether, they moved like lightning—fast, coordinated, deadly.

Kaelen met Berenger in the center of the road, and the clash of their swords sounded like a thunderclap.

"You were my brother!" Berenger hissed, pressing his blade down with the kind of strength that came from years of discipline and absolute conviction. The Holy Light radiating from his weapon began to singe the edges of Kaelen's gambeson.

"Then you should have told me the truth," Kaelen retorted. He didn't use a holy strike—didn't have access to that power anymore, didn't want it even if he did. Instead, he used a low, dirty kick to Berenger's knee—a move the Order considered "beneath" a knight but that was devastatingly effective.

Berenger stumbled, and Kaelen followed up with a hilt-smash to the side of his mentor's helmet, the impact reverberating up his arm.

In the chaos around them, the battle raged. The spectral soldiers fought with the muscle memory of their living years, and the Purifiers—for all their training, for all their blessed armor—had never faced an enemy that couldn't be killed because it was already dead.

One of the Purifiers broke through the skeletal line, his blessed spear leveled directly at Elara's chest. She saw it coming, tried to dodge, but her exhaustion made her slow—

"ELARA!" Kaelen's heart didn't just stop; it exploded with pure, primal terror.

He didn't think. Didn't calculate the tactical disadvantage. He threw his sword—his primary weapon, his only real defense—and the silver blade spun through the air in a perfect arc.

It caught the Purifier in the shoulder joint just as he lunged, the impact throwing off his aim. But momentum carried the spear forward, and Kaelen was already moving, his body a shield of scarred steel interposing itself between the blade and Elara.

The Sun-Fire spear bit deep into the gap in Kaelen's armor, right at the ribs where the plate didn't quite overlap.

Pain exploded through him—not just the physical agony of steel piercing flesh, but the burning, caustic heat of concentrated holy fire eating into his body from the inside.

Through the tether, Elara felt it all. Felt his ribs crack. Felt the poison spreading. Felt his heart stutter and his breath catch and his absolute, bone-deep refusal to let her die even if it meant his own death.

"NO!" The scream that tore from Elara's throat wasn't human. It was the sound of something fundamental breaking, of a woman who had finally found someone worth living for watching him die to protect her.

The explosion of pink magic that followed was less a spell and more a shockwave.

Every ghost on the field let out a synchronized shriek that shattered the Purifiers' visors, the neon light so bright it turned the grey mist into something that looked like the aftermath of a star going supernova. The Purifiers reeled back, blinded and disoriented, their formation breaking.

"RETREAT!" one of them shouted. "The witch is too strong! Fall back to the rally point!"

They fled into the mist, dragging their wounded, leaving behind broken weapons and the smell of ozone and fear.

Berenger went with them, casting one last look at Kaelen—a look that held grief and fury and the terrible realization that the boy he'd trained had chosen his own path, even if it led to damnation.

Elara was at Kaelen's side before they'd even disappeared, her hands already glowing as she pressed them against the wound in his side. He was slumped against the boulder, his breath coming in shallow, wet rasps that spoke of punctured lung and internal bleeding.

The wound wasn't bleeding red. It was smoking with white, caustic heat—Sun-Fire poisoning spreading through his chest like frost.

"Who did this to you?" she whispered, her voice trembling with a rage so deep it felt like the earth itself was shaking. The question wasn't gentle. It was a threat. A promise of violence against anyone who had dared harm what was hers.

"Berenger," Kaelen managed through gritted teeth. His hand found hers, squeezed weakly. "And... the High Priest who gave... the order."

Elara nodded once, her face hardening into an expression that would have made the Purifiers reconsider their entire career path.

"Good," she said quietly, her magic already working to stabilize him, to keep him breathing long enough to get somewhere she could actually heal him. "I was hoping you'd say that. Because I am a monster, Kaelen. I am the thing they warn children about. And I am going to show them exactly why you should never, ever try to kill what belongs to me."

She hauled him up, his arm over her shoulder, the silver tether between them pulsing red with warning and agony. Cinder appeared from wherever he'd fled during the battle, his eyes rolling but his loyalty absolute.

"We need to move," Elara gasped. "The Deep Woods. There's a place—old magic, older than the Order. They won't follow us there."

"Cannot… make it…" Kaelen's eyes were starting to flutter closed.

"Yes, you can," Elara commanded, her voice taking on that deadly authority she used when forcing spirits to obey. "You're Sir Kaelen. You chose me over your god. You threw away everything to stand with me. You don't get to die now. You don't get to leave me alone. So you're going to stay conscious, you're going to get on that horse, and you're going to let me save you the way you saved me."

Through the tether, through the agony, Kaelen felt her absolute refusal to let him go. Felt her love—fierce and possessive and utterly unshakable.

"Bossy," he mumbled, but he let her help him onto Cinder's back.

"Damn right," she replied, swinging up behind him, her arms wrapping around his waist to keep him upright. "Now hold on, because we're about to have a very interesting few days in the woods, and I need you alive to complain about it."

They rode into the Deep Woods as the mist closed behind them like a curtain, hiding them from the Purifiers who would surely come looking.

Behind them, the ghosts faded back into the earth, their job done.

Ahead, the trees waited—dark and wild and dangerous, but safer than the false light of the Order.

And between them, the silver tether pulsed with determination.

They would survive this. They would expose the truth. They would burn the Cathedral down.

But first, Elara had to keep the man she loved breathing long enough to see it happen.

Chapter Fourteen

THE HUNTED

The forest didn't welcome them. It swallowed them whole.

Elara half-ran, half-dragged Kaelen through the underbrush, her boots slipping on moss-slick roots as the Deep Woods closed in around them like a fist. Behind them, she could still hear the Purifiers—distant shouts, the metallic clang of armor, the unmistakable hiss of Holy Light being channeled through blessed steel.

"Keep moving," she hissed, her arm locked around Kaelen's waist as he stumbled. "Kaelen, stay with me. Just a little further."

"Cannot," he rasped, his weight growing heavier with each step. His face was grey beneath the dirt and blood, his skin slick with a cold sweat that had nothing to do with exertion. "Elara… leave me. Take Cinder and—"

"Finish that sentence and I'll kill you myself," she snapped, though her voice cracked on the last word. The silver tether at her wrist was pulsing erratically—red, then grey, then a sickly, flickering white that made her stomach clench with fear.

He was dying. The Sun-Fire spear that had pierced his ribs wasn't just a wound; it was an infection. The crystalline white poison was spreading through his chest like frost, turning his blood to liquid light that burned him from the inside out.

She could feel it through the tether—the agony radiating from the wound site, the way his heartbeat was starting to skip and stutter like a damaged clock.

Cinder crashed through the brambles behind them, his eyes rolling white with terror. The warhorse hated the Deep Woods— hated the way the trees seemed to lean in and whisper, hated the cold spots where spirits lingered in the shadows. But he followed anyway, loyal to the man who was currently bleeding to death in Elara's arms.

"Arthur!" Elara screamed into the gloom. "I need eyes ahead! Find us shelter!"

A translucent blur of indignation materialized beside her, the ghost of Sir Arthur flickering in and out of visibility as he struggled to maintain form in the hostile atmosphere of the woods.

"There are wards here, girl," Arthur wheezed, his mustache drooping with the effort of staying corporeal. "Old ones. Primal. The spirits in these woods don't like the living, and they certainly don't appreciate the flashy, neon-pink variety of necromancer barging through their territory."

"I don't care if they're hosting a spectral tea party," Elara snarled, adjusting her grip on Kaelen as he sagged against her. "Find. Us. Shelter. Now."

Arthur's translucent form shimmered with offense, but he vanished into the tree line without another word.

Elara kept moving. Each step was a negotiation with gravity and willpower. Kaelen was easily twice her weight in armor alone, and even with the breastplate abandoned in the chaos of their escape, he was still a wall of muscle and stubborn, dying paladin.

"Talk to me," she demanded, her breath coming in ragged gasps. "Kaelen, tell me something. Anything. Don't you dare go silent on me."

"You're... bossy," he managed, a ghost of his usual gruffness threading through the pain. "Did anyone... ever tell you that?"

"Constantly. It's one of my most charming qualities." She shoved a low-hanging branch out of their path, her magic flaring pink to light the darkening woods. "What else?"

"Your hair... is in my mouth."

"Romantic."

"Tastes like... graveyard dirt and... peonies."

Despite everything—despite the blood seeping through her fingers where she gripped his side, despite the Purifiers somewhere behind them, despite the fact that the man she'd accidentally fallen in love with was quite literally poisoned by the god he'd served his entire life—Elara laughed. It was a sharp, half-hysterical sound, but it was real.

"When we get out of this," she said, her voice fierce, "I'm going to make you take a proper bath. With soap. Possibly supervision."

"Looking forward... to it," Kaelen wheezed. Then his knees buckled.

Elara went down with him, both of them crashing into the undergrowth in a tangle of limbs and silver thread. The tether flared red—a warning she didn't need. His heart was failing.

"No," she gasped, rolling him onto his back. "No, no, no. Kaelen, open your eyes. Look at me."

His eyelids fluttered. The whites of his eyes were threaded with those same white, crystalline veins—the Sun-Fire eating through him like acid through paper.

She pressed her hands to the wound in his side. The moment her skin made contact with the infection, pain exploded up her arms—a searing, holy agony that felt like every nerve ending in her body was being set on fire. She screamed, jerking back instinctively.

"Don't... touch it," Kaelen managed, his hand weakly catching her wrist. "Burns you. S'not worth—"

"Shut up," she said, tears streaming down her face. "Just shut up and let me think."

But there was no time to think. The forest around them was growing darker, the shadows deepening into something thick and hungry. She could feel the Purifiers getting closer—their Light like a distant, artificial sun cutting through the natural gloom.

"Girl!" Arthur's voice cut through the panic. The ghost materialized directly in front of her, his usual pompous expression replaced with something almost gentle. "There's a hollow. Lightning-struck oak, two hundred yards north-northwest. Big enough for the horse. Defensible."

"Can you carry him?" Elara asked, already knowing the answer.

"I'm a ghost, not a carthorse," Arthur said, but his tone was softer than usual. "But I can scout the path. Make sure nothing spectral tries to eat you on the way."

"Good enough." Elara grabbed Kaelen under the arms, her muscles screaming in protest. "Kaelen, I need you to stand. Just one more time. I'll do the rest, but I need you vertical."

"Cannot."

"You can," she said, her voice dropping into a register she usually reserved for commanding the stubborn dead. "You're Sir Kaelen, the Golden Lion, the man who threw away his entire life to save mine. You don't get to quit now. Stand. Up."

Something in her tone—maybe the authority, maybe the desperation, maybe the fact that the silver tether was practically vibrating with her refusal to let him go—got through. Kaelen's eyes opened, clearer for just a moment.

"Bossy," he repeated.

"Damn right. Now move."

He moved.

. . .

The journey to the hollow took a lifetime compressed into twenty minutes.

Elara half-carried, half-dragged Kaelen through the underbrush, following Arthur's flickering form as the ghost darted between trees, scouting for threats. Cinder followed close behind, his warm breath on her neck a small comfort in the oppressive darkness.

The Deep Woods were living up to their name. The trees here were ancient—so old their trunks were wider than houses, their roots erupting from the soil in gnarled, serpentine tangles that seemed designed to trip the unwary. The canopy overhead was so thick that even the fading daylight couldn't penetrate, leaving everything in a perpetual, greenish twilight.

And the spirits here were wrong.

Elara could feel them watching—not the gentle, curious dead she was used to, but something older. Primal. These weren't human ghosts; they were the echoes of the forest itself, the memory of trees that had been felled, of animals that had died screaming in traps, of blood soaked so deep into the earth that it had become part of the landscape's soul.

They didn't like her. And they really didn't like Kaelen.

"Almost there," Arthur called back, his voice thin and strained. "Just past this thicket—gods, girl, what did you do to anger every dead thing in a ten-mile radius?"

"It's not me," Elara gasped, her arms burning with the effort of keeping Kaelen upright. "It's him. They can smell the Light on him. To them, he's… he's poison."

"Ironic," Arthur muttered, "considering he's currently being poisoned by said Light."

"Not. Helping."

They burst through a final curtain of hanging moss and stumbled into the hollow. It was exactly as Arthur had described—a massive oak tree, its trunk split down the middle by some ancient lightning strike, creating a cave-like space just big enough for a horse and two desperate humans.

Elara practically threw Kaelen inside, then turned to grab Cinder's reins. The horse balked, his ears flat against his skull.

"I know," she told him, her voice gentle despite the panic clawing at her throat. "I know it's scary. But he needs you. We both need you. Please."

Cinder's dark eyes met hers. For a moment, she saw a flicker of something—not intelligence, exactly, but understanding. The horse had carried Kaelen through a dozen battles. He'd stood steady while his rider dispensed the Order's brutal justice. He'd tolerated ghosts and necromancers and the end of the world as he knew it.

He could tolerate this.

The warhorse ducked his head and stepped into the hollow, pressing himself against the back wall to make room. Elara followed, collapsing beside Kaelen in the dirt.

The moment they were inside, Arthur flickered to the entrance, his translucent form spreading thin to cover the opening like a curtain.

"I'll keep watch," he said. "If those Purifiers get close, I'll… I'll think of something appropriately terrifying."

"Arthur—"

"Save him, girl," the ghost said quietly. "We can argue about my heroism later."

Then he was gone, his presence a faint shimmer at the mouth of the hollow.

Elara turned to Kaelen. In the dim, filtered light, he looked like a corpse. His lips were blue, his breathing shallow and irregular. The wound in his side had stopped bleeding, but only because the Sun-Fire had cauterized it from within. Through the torn fabric of his tunic, she could see the infection spreading—white, crystalline veins radiating from the impact site like a spider's web.

"Kaelen," she whispered, her hands hovering over him, afraid to touch and cause more pain. "I don't know how to fix this. I don't know how to stop it."

His eyes cracked open, just a sliver of gold amid the white. "Don't," he rasped. "Don't try. Too dangerous. You said... holy fire burns necromancers. This is... concentrated divinity. If you try to pull it out..."

"What, I'll die?" Elara laughed, the sound brittle and sharp. "Kaelen, the tether means if you die, I die anyway. So either we both live, or we both go. Those are the options."

"Elara—"

"No," she said, her voice dropping into that deadly calm she'd used in the graveyard when she'd first threatened to wake an army. "No more arguing. No more noble sacrifice. You chose me over the Order. You threw away your vows, your brothers, your entire life for me. So now I'm choosing you. And I am very, very good at getting what I want."

She leaned over him, her dark hair falling around them like a curtain, the neon-pink strands scattered through it glowing softly in the dim light. In the dim hollow, her eyes glowed with that familiar, defiant light—the same light that had made him stop in the graveyard all those weeks ago, the same light that had haunted his dreams and shattered his certainties.

"Who did this to you?" she whispered, her fingers tracing the air above the wound without touching. The question wasn't soft or gentle. It was a threat. A promise of violence.

"Berenger," Kaelen managed. "And… the High Priest."

Elara nodded once, her expression hardening into something that would have made the Purifiers think twice about their life choices.

"Good," she said quietly. "I was hoping you'd say that. Because I am a monster, Kaelen. I am the thing they warn children about in bedtime stories. And I am going to show them exactly why you should never, ever try to kill what belongs to me."

She pressed her palms flat against his chest, right over the spreading infection.

And then she reached for the deepest, darkest part of her power—the part she usually kept locked away because it scared even her.

The part that didn't just speak to death.

The part that could command it.

Chapter Fifteen

THE VIOLET FIRE

The transformation didn't start with light. It started with absence.

The neon-pink glow that usually surrounded Elara's hands flickered and died, snuffed out like a candle in a hurricane. For one terrible, breathless moment, the hollow went completely dark. Even the faint luminescence of the Deep Woods' spectral presences seemed to retreat, as if whatever Elara was about to do required privacy.

Then the violet came.

It didn't glow—it pulled. It was the color of a bruise, of the space between stars, of the exact moment before a storm breaks. It seeped from Elara's skin like smoke, coiling around her arms in serpentine ribbons that hissed when they touched the air.

Kaelen tried to pull away. Every instinct he'd been trained with screamed that this was wrong, that this was the corruption the Order had warned about, that this was the moment Elara would tip over the edge into the abyss.

But the silver tether held him fast. And more than that—through their shared connection, he felt her intention. This wasn't corruption. This was control. Absolute, terrifying, breathtaking control.

"Elara," he gasped, his voice barely a whisper. "What are you doing?"

"Saving you," she said. Her eyes had changed. The neon-pink was still there, but now it was rimmed with violet—a dark corona that made her look less like a girl playing with death and more like death itself had decided to wear her skin.

She didn't reach for a spell. She didn't speak to the spirits. She reached through the tether—through their shared soul-bond—and she grabbed hold of the Sun-Fire poison in his chest.

The pain was immediate and absolute.

Elara screamed—a raw, primal sound that sent every bird in the canopy exploding into flight. Through the tether, Kaelen felt what she was experiencing, and it was agony condensed into its purest form.

The Sun-Fire wasn't just burning her. It was trying to unmake her. It recognized her as its opposite—life in death, shadow where there should be light—and it wanted to erase her from existence with the zealous fury of a fanatic destroying a heretic.

But Elara didn't let go.

She pulled.

The white, crystalline infection began to move, dragged out of Kaelen's flesh by sheer force of will. It didn't want to go. It had been designed to spread, to consume, to purify everything it touched until nothing remained but sterile, holy emptiness.

Elara was stronger.

The violet magic around her hands darkened to near-black, forming a void that was somehow more present than absence. She was using her necromancy not to commune with death, but to create it—a space where the Sun-Fire's existence simply wasn't allowed.

"I am the woman who keeps the keys to the gate," she hissed through gritted teeth, her voice overlapping with something older and far more terrifying. "And you are not welcome here."

The Sun-Fire came out of Kaelen's chest in a single, jagged spike of crystallized light. It was beautiful and horrible—a shard of pure, concentrated divinity that looked like a sword made of dawn itself.

Elara caught it in her bare hands.

The moment her skin touched it, her palms began to burn. Not metaphorically—they actually caught fire. Holy fire. The kind that was supposed to reduce necromancers to ash and screaming.

She held on anyway.

Through the tether, Kaelen felt her pain, and it was worse than anything he'd experienced on the battlefield. It was the sensation of being unmade at the molecular level, of every cell in her hands deciding simultaneously that existing was no longer an option.

"Elara, let go!" he shouted, trying to reach for her, but his body wouldn't obey. The removal of the Sun-Fire had left him weak as a newborn, his limbs trembling with the effort just to breathe.

"Not. Yet." Her voice was barely human now, layered with harmonics that sounded like a choir of the dead singing in reverse.

She closed her fists around the spike of light.

The violet magic surged, wrapping around the Sun-Fire like a serpent constricting prey. For a moment, the two forces were locked in stalemate—light and void, life and death, Order and chaos. The air in the hollow began to crack, reality itself straining under the pressure of two fundamental forces trying to occupy the same space.

Then Elara did something that should have been impossible.

She absorbed it.

Not destroyed it, not dispelled it, not redirected it. She pulled the Sun-Fire into herself, into the vast, hungry void of her necromantic power, and she swallowed it whole.

The explosion of energy that followed wasn't an explosion at all. It was an implosion—a sudden, violent sucking of all heat and light and sound into a single point in Elara's chest.

She went rigid, her back arching, her mouth open in a silent scream. The violet magic around her flared so bright it bleached the color from the walls of the hollow, turning everything into stark black-and-white negative.

And then, just as suddenly, it was over.

Elara collapsed forward onto Kaelen's chest, gasping for air. The violet magic faded back to her usual neon-pink, then dimmed to almost nothing. Her hands, still pressed against Kaelen's ribs, were blackened and blistered—the skin cracked and weeping with burns that went deeper than flesh.

But the Sun-Fire was gone.

Where the wound had been in Kaelen's side, there was now only a scar. Not a neat, surgical line, but a jagged, brutal mark in the exact shape of Elara's handprint—burned into his skin in rose-gold, as if she'd branded him with her own life-force.

"Elara," Kaelen breathed, his hands coming up to cradle her even though his entire body felt like it had been wrung out and left to dry. "What did you do?"

"Saved you," she mumbled into his chest, her voice small and exhausted. "Told you I would."

"You could have died."

"So could you." She tilted her head up, and despite the exhaustion, despite the pain radiating from her burned hands, her eyes still held that familiar, defiant spark. "I told you, Kaelen. We both live, or we both go. I meant it."

He looked at her hands—at the blackened, ruined skin—and something in his chest cracked open. Not the wound. Something deeper. The last, carefully maintained wall between duty and desire, between what he was supposed to be and what he actually was.

She'd asked him in the darkness: "Who did this to you?" Her voice a promise of violence.

Now it was his turn.

Kaelen sat up slowly, every muscle screaming in protest, cradling her against him. His hand was gentle as he examined the damage to her palms. The burns were severe—third degree at least, possibly worse. The skin was blackened and cracked, weeping fluid that should have been blood but instead glowed faintly pink.

She wouldn't be able to use her hands for days, maybe weeks.

And she'd done it anyway. Without hesitation. Without calculating the cost.

For him.

"Who did this to you?" he asked, his voice so quiet it was almost a whisper, but the fury underneath it was molten. Through the tether, Elara could feel it—a rage so deep and cold it felt like the ocean floor, dark and crushing and absolute.

"Berenger," Elara said, meeting his eyes. "And the High Priest who gave the order."

Kaelen's jaw tightened. His hand moved to the rose-gold handprint scarred into his ribs—her mark on him, permanent and possessive. Through the tether, she felt his emotions shift from fury to something that felt like awe, like devotion, like a vow being taken in the silence of his own heart.

"Then I suppose we'd better make sure they regret it," Elara said, her answering smile sharp enough to cut.

"I'm not letting them walk away from this," Kaelen said. It wasn't a threat. It was a statement of fact, delivered with the calm certainty of a man who had finally stopped lying to himself about who he was. "I'm going to tear that Cathedral down brick by blessed brick. I'm going to show the world what they did. And when I'm done, there won't be enough left of the High Priest to bury."

"That's the spirit," Elara said, wincing as she tried to flex her fingers and failed. "Though maybe we table the vengeance until I can actually hold a shovel again."

Kaelen carefully began tearing strips from his tunic, his movements practiced despite the trembling in his hands. He'd done field dressings a hundred times before—for his men, for strangers, for causes he no longer believed in.

This was different. This was holy work.

"Does it hurt?" he asked softly, wrapping the first strip around her palm with impossible gentleness.

"Like I shoved my hands into the sun," Elara admitted, her voice tight with pain she was trying to hide. "But I'd do it again. In a heartbeat."

"I know you would," Kaelen said, and there was something raw in his voice. "That's what terrifies me. You don't hesitate. You don't calculate the cost. You just... act. Like my life is worth more than yours."

"It is to me," Elara said simply.

"Elara—"

"No." Her good hand—well, her less-damaged hand—reached up to cup his face, forcing him to look at her. "You don't get to argue about this. You threw yourself in front of a spear for me. You gave up everything—your Order, your brothers, your entire identity—to stand with me. So don't you dare tell me I'm not allowed to save you back."

Through the tether, Kaelen felt the truth of it. Felt her fierce, possessive love. Felt the way she'd rather burn herself to ash than watch him die.

Felt, for the first time in his life, what it meant to be chosen. Not because of duty or vows or what he could offer. Just... chosen. For himself.

"The scar," Elara said, her eyes dropping to the handprint burned into his ribs. "I'm sorry. I didn't mean to mark you like that."

"Don't be." Kaelen's hand covered the scar, feeling the raised, warm tissue. Even now, hours after the healing, it radiated a gentle heat—her magic, permanently written into his skin. "It's a reminder."

"Of what?"

"That I was worth saving." He looked at her, really looked at her—at the dark hair now matted with sweat and dirt, the scattered pink strands still faintly luminous among the brown, at the exhaustion written in every line of her face, at the woman who had just done the impossible to keep him alive. "That you chose me. Even when it cost you everything."

Elara's breath hitched. The banter, the sarcasm, the carefully maintained armor of humor—it all fell away, leaving only raw, terrifying honesty.

"I didn't choose you because it was easy, Kaelen," she whispered. "I chose you because I'm selfish. Because the thought of a world without you in it felt like death. And I know death intimately. I speak to it every day. But this—losing you—that would have been different. That would have been the kind of death I couldn't come back from."

The words hung in the air between them, heavier than any vow, more binding than any tether.

Kaelen finished wrapping her hands in silence, his touch reverent. When he was done, he didn't pull away. Instead, he cradled her bandaged hands in his, bringing them to his lips in a gesture so tender it made her chest ache.

"I don't have the words," he said quietly. "I don't know how to say what I feel. The Order trained me to be a weapon, not a man. I don't know how to do this—how to love someone without destroying them or myself in the process."

"Then don't say anything," Elara said, leaning into him. "Just... stay. Be here. With me."

He kissed her then. Not the desperate, frantic press of lips from before, but something slower. Deeper. A kiss that tasted of salt and ash and promises neither of them was entirely sure they could keep.

When they pulled apart, the hollow felt different. Warmer, somehow, despite the cold of the Deep Woods pressing in around them.

"We should rest," Kaelen said reluctantly, even as his arms tightened around her. "You're exhausted, and I'm—"

"Recovering from having holy poison ripped out of your chest?" Elara supplied helpfully. "Yes, you're very weak and fragile. Practically a delicate flower."

"I was going to say 'grateful,'" he corrected, a smile tugging at his lips despite everything. "But I'll take 'delicate flower' if it gets you to actually sleep for once."

"I don't sleep," Elara protested, even as her eyelids drooped. "I'm a necromancer. We're nocturnal. It's in the job description."

"Elara."

"Fine. But only because you're injured and I'm too tired to argue properly."

She settled against him, careful of his newly-scarred ribs, her head resting over his heart. The steady thud-thud-thud of it was the most beautiful sound she'd ever heard—proof that he was alive, that they'd both made it through.

Through the tether, she could feel his emotions—exhaustion, yes, but also peace. A quiet contentment that he probably hadn't felt since before the Order got their hands on him as a child.

Outside the hollow, Arthur's voice drifted back to them, a faint whisper in the darkness.

"They're turning back. The Purifiers. They think you're dead—there was too much blood on the trail. They're reporting a successful kill."

"Good," Kaelen called back softly. "Let them think we're dead. It'll make the resurrection more dramatic."

Elara laughed against his chest, the sound muffled and half-asleep. "You're learning, Sir Kaelen. Give it another week and I'll have you making jokes about corpses."

"I'm already bound to one," he pointed out. "Might as well embrace it."

"That was actually good," Elara mumbled, her words slurring with exhaustion. "I'm proud of you."

"Go to sleep, Elara."

"Bossy."

"I learned from the best."

The banter faded into comfortable silence. Through the tether, they could feel each other's heartbeat synchronizing, their breathing falling into rhythm. Two broken pieces that somehow fit together better than either of them had ever fit into the world they'd been born into.

In the back of the hollow, Cinder shifted, his dark eyes watchful but calm. The warhorse had seen his rider through a dozen battles, had carried him through fire and blood and the collapse of everything Kaelen had believed in.

This—two humans tangled together in the dirt, choosing each other over duty and dogma and every law that said they shouldn't—was the first thing that had made sense in a very long time.

Tomorrow, they would begin the journey to the Grey Wastes. Tomorrow, they would plan a revolution. Tomorrow, they would show the High Order what happened when you tried to kill the wrong monster.

But tonight, in a hollow tree in the Deep Woods, with a loyal horse standing guard and a pompous ghost keeping watch, they were simply alive.

And for two people who'd spent their entire lives negotiating with death, that was more than enough.

Chapter Sixteen

THE SOUL-ANCHOR

The silence of the Deep Woods was no longer empty; it was heavy, filled with the thrumming resonance of two souls forced into the same frequency.

Elara lay draped across Kaelen's chest, her breathing shallow and jagged. The handprint scar she had burned into his ribs pulsed with a faint, rose-gold light—a permanent reminder of the death she had pulled out of him. Her own hands were blistered black from absorbing the Sun-Fire poison, the skin cracked and weeping a faint, pink luminescence.

To save him, she hadn't just moved the poison. She had opened a door between them that didn't have a lock.

The silver tether wasn't a glowing wire anymore. It had expanded into a shimmering, translucent veil that wrapped around them both like a cocoon of fuchsia and gold. The air inside the makeshift shelter shimmered with residual magic, thick enough to taste—copper and peonies and something ancient that neither of them had words for.

"Kaelen," she whispered, but her voice didn't come from her throat. It echoed inside his mind, intimate and terrifying.

Don't look, Kaelen's internal voice pleaded, raw with panic. Elara, please. Stay in the present. Don't go deeper.

But the anchor had been dropped. The weight of their shared magic dragged them down into the dark water of memory, and neither of them had the strength left to fight the current.

Elara felt it first—the sensation of falling backward through time, her consciousness slipping through the cracks in Kaelen's carefully constructed armor. The forest around them began to fade, replaced by cold stone and the smell of incense so thick it choked.

"No," Kaelen gasped aloud, his physical body jerking beneath her. "Elara, pull back. You don't want to see this."

But she was already there.

∘ ∘ ∘

KAELEN'S MEMORY: THE FORGE OF THE LION

Suddenly, they weren't in the woods.

They were in the High Cathedral, fourteen years ago. The air tasted of winter and iron and a terror so profound it had soaked into the very stones. Everything was too big, too bright, too cold.

Elara watched through Kaelen's younger eyes—a ten-year-old boy's eyes. His hands were small, raw and bleeding from clutching a practice sword for twelve hours straight. His shoulders ached with a bone-deep exhaustion that no child should know. Before him stood the High Priest Valerius, though he looked different here—younger, but no less cruel. He looked less like a servant of God and more like a statue carved from spite and winter.

"The Light does not negotiate with the flesh, Kaelen," the Priest's voice rang out, cold as a winter grave. Each word landed like a physical blow on the boy's skin. "Your father died a coward because he felt 'pity' for the fallen. He let his weakness infect his duty. Do you wish to be a coward like him?"

"No, Eminence," the boy whispered. His voice was so small. So terrified.

Elara felt the wave of nauseating horror that rolled through young Kaelen—the grief for his father barely six months buried, the desperate need to please these men who were now his only family, the bone-deep certainty that if he failed this test, there would be nowhere left for him to go.

"Then prove it," Valerius said, stepping aside.

In the courtyard beyond the archway, a small bundle of orange fur huddled against the cold stone. A cat. Scrawny, malnourished, with one ear torn from a past fight. But its eyes were bright and trusting as it looked toward the boy.

Barnaby, Elara heard Kaelen's child-voice whisper in his mind. His name is Barnaby. I found him in the stables. I gave him my breakfast scraps for three weeks. He purrs when I scratch behind his good ear. He sleeps on my feet when the dormitory is cold.

"The animal is blighted by shadow," Valerius continued, his voice devoid of any warmth. "It carries the taint of the natural world—corruption, chaos, attachment to base desires. These are the things that destroy paladins, Kaelen. Affection. Mercy. Love. They are weapons our enemies use against us."

The boy's hands were shaking. "He's just a cat, Eminence. He's not hurting anyone. He—"

"He is a test." Valerius placed a hand on the boy's shoulder, the grip bruising. "Your father failed his test. He chose compassion over duty, and it cost him his life and nearly damned his soul. You will not make the same mistake. Purge it."

Young Kaelen looked down at his hands. They were so small. The sword they pressed into his grip was too heavy, the pommel still warm from the training yard. Behind him, he could hear the other recruits watching from the shadows—twenty pairs of eyes witnessing his weakness, his hesitation, waiting to see if he would break.

The cat meowed. A soft, trusting sound.

Please, the boy's mind screamed. Please don't make me do this. I'll do anything else. I'll train harder. I'll pray longer. I'll—

"Purge it," Valerius repeated, and there was no mercy in his voice. "Or join your father in his coward's grave."

Kaelen's small hands tightened on the sword.

He took one step forward. Then another.

Barnaby purred, recognizing his friend. The cat rubbed against his ankle, tail up, completely trusting.

The boy closed his eyes.

The sword came down.

The memory didn't show the impact. It didn't need to. Elara felt the moment the light went out of the small, warm body. Felt young Kaelen's soul crack like ice on a winter pond—a fracture that would never fully heal.

The boy didn't cry. He couldn't. Valerius was watching. The recruits were watching. He turned his face into a mask—blank, obedient, empty—and handed the bloodied sword back to his teacher.

"Well done," Valerius said, and the approval in his voice was worse than any punishment. "You have passed the first trial. The weakness is purged. Now you can begin to become what the Light requires."

The boy nodded, mute and hollow.

That night, locked in the dormitory alone, he buried his face in his thin pillow and screamed until his voice broke. He built the armor around his heart piece by piece—gold and duty and righteous purpose—until he couldn't remember what it felt like to love something small and fragile.

Until Elara.

The adult Kaelen's shame washed over her in the present, a bitter, acidic tide that burned worse than the Sun-Fire. *That is what they made me,* his mind whispered to hers. *A killer of small things in the name of a Great Light. A statue. A weapon. A coward who chose survival over mercy.*

No, Elara's consciousness pushed back, fierce and absolute. *A child who was tortured into obedience. A boy who survived the only way he could.*

. . .

ELARA'S MEMORY: THE LONELINESS OF THE PEONY

The scene shifted violently, tearing them out of the Cathedral's cold stone. The world tilted, and suddenly everything was warm.

Too warm. Summer-warm. Death-warm.

They were in a small, sun-drenched cottage on the edge of a cliff. The air smelled of salt water and rotting flowers—peonies past their prime, browning at the edges, petals falling like tears onto a wooden table.

Kaelen was the observer now, thrust into Elara's seven-year-old perspective. Everything was too bright, too loud, too full of a desperate, clawing grief that didn't have words yet.

A woman lay in the bed by the window. Her hair was silver-white, her hands folded across her chest in the stillness that only came after the last breath had rattled free. Elara's grandmother. The only person in the entire world who had ever looked at the strange, pink-eyed child and seen something other than a curse.

Seven-year-old Elara sat beside the bed, her small hand clutching her grandmother's cold fingers. She wasn't crying. She was talking.

"The tea is still warm, Grandma," the little girl said, her voice bright with a desperate, fragile hope. "I made it just how you like it. Two lumps of sugar. I didn't spill any this time."

Beside the bed, shimmering in the afternoon light, a grey, flickering shape sat in the rocking chair. It was the grandmother—or what was left of her. A ghost in the making, her eyes still closed, her form not quite solid yet. The old woman's spirit hadn't realized it was dead yet. She was still reaching for the living world, confused and fading.

"Elara, sweetheart," the ghost whispered, her voice like wind through paper. "Why cannot I feel the teacup?"

"Because you're not thirsty anymore, Grandma," young Elara said, her tone patient and matter-of-fact in the way only children could be when explaining the incomprehensible. "You don't need to eat or drink now. But you can still stay. You can stay as long as you want."

Kaelen felt the child's desperate loneliness—a crushing, suffocating weight that no seven-year-old should carry. Her parents had died in a fishing accident when she was three. Her grandmother was all she had left. The village called her "Ghoul-Girl" and "Witch-Spawn" and threw stones at her when she walked to the market.

She didn't want to be a necromancer. She just didn't want to be alone.

Through the window, Kaelen could see the village children gathering at the garden gate. They were pointing, their faces twisted with a mix of fear and cruelty that children learned from their parents.

"Freak!" one of them shouted, his voice high and mocking. "The Witch-Child is talking to the air again!"

"She's making the dead walk!" another yelled. "My ma says she's cursed! Says she'll bring the plague!"

A stone flew through the window, shattering the glass. It hit the wall beside young Elara's head, missing her by inches. She didn't flinch. She was used to it.

"Why don't you join her in the dirt, Ghoul-Girl?" a third child screamed, and the others laughed—that terrible, bright laughter of young cruelty that didn't yet understand the weight of its own violence.

Young Elara turned her back on them. She climbed into the bed beside her grandmother's body and curled up against the cooling flesh, her small arms wrapped around the only person who had ever loved her.

"I don't care what they say, Grandma," she whispered into the silence. "I like the quiet ones better anyway. The living are too loud. They don't listen. But you always listened."

The ghost in the rocking chair flickered, growing fainter. "Elara, my darling girl… I think I have to go now. I can hear something calling me. It sounds like… like home."

"No!" The child's voice cracked, the careful composure shattering. "You cannot go! You promised you wouldn't leave me! You promised!"

"I'm not leaving you, sweetheart. I'm just… changing. But I'll always be close. In the earth. In the roots. In every peony that blooms."

"I don't want peonies!" young Elara sobbed, her face pressed against her grandmother's shoulder. "I want you!"

But the ghost was already fading, her form dissolving into a soft, pink mist that settled over the little girl like a benediction. And in that moment, Elara made a choice.

If the living wouldn't love her, she would love the dead.

If the world called her a monster for seeing ghosts, she would become the best damn monster they'd ever seen.

She would be loud, bright, impossible to ignore. She would wear lace and neon-pink and smile with all her teeth. She would make them look at her and see power instead of pity.

She would never, ever let them see how much it hurt to be alone.

Kaelen felt her crushing loneliness—the years of isolation that followed, the weight of every conversation held with spirits instead of friends, the desperate, aching need to be touched, to be seen, to matter to someone who was still breathing.

Until Kaelen.

I see you, Kaelen's mind breathed into hers, the words a vow. Elara, I see you. Not the monster. Not the witch. I see the girl who loved her grandmother. I see the woman who saved me. I see you.

* * *

THE SHARED PRESENT

The forest rushed back with the force of a thunderclap.

Elara gasped, her eyes snapping open. She was staring directly into Kaelen's golden irises, their faces so close she could count the individual shards of amber in his eyes. They were both weeping— hot, silent tears that carved paths through the grime on their faces.

The tether settled between them, no longer a violent, whipping storm. It pulsed with a steady, rhythmic glow—white-gold, rose-pink, silver, all the colors of their combined souls braided together into something new.

They were no longer two people tied together by a curse. They were two broken halves of a truth the world had tried to burn.

"Barnaby," Elara whispered, her voice raw. Her hand moved to cup his cheek, her burned palm gentle against his stubbled jaw. "His name was Barnaby. And he purred when you scratched behind his good ear."

Kaelen's breath hitched, a sound caught between a laugh and a sob. He closed his eyes, leaning into her touch as if she were the only thing keeping him tethered to the earth. "And your grandmother… she liked two lumps of sugar. Even when she was a ghost."

The vulnerability was absolute. The armor was gone. There were no more secrets, no more carefully constructed lies. He knew her shame, and she knew his bloodstains, and neither of them had looked away.

"We cannot go back," Kaelen said, his voice stronger now, though his hand still trembled as it found hers. The silver tether hummed between them, warm and alive. "Not just because of the truth we carry. Because of this. Because of us."

"We were never going back, Kaelen," Elara said, a familiar, defiant spark returning to her neon-pink eyes. She sat up, pulling him with her, their movements synchronized in a way that no longer felt like coincidence. "We're going forward. To the Capital. To the Cathedral. And we're going to show them that the Lion has teeth and the Witch has an army."

Kaelen looked at the handprint scar on his ribs—the permanent mark she had left when she pulled death out of him. He reached out and took her burned hands in his, pressing a kiss to each scarred palm.

"The scar," Elara said, her eyes dropping to the handprint burned into his ribs. "I'm sorry. I didn't mean to mark you like that."

"Don't be." Kaelen's hand covered the scar, feeling the raised, warm tissue. "It's a reminder."

"Of what?"

"That I was worth saving." He looked at her, really looked at her—at the dark hair now matted with sweat and dirt, pink strands still glowing faintly through it, at the exhaustion written in every line of her face, at the woman who had just done the impossible to keep him alive. "That you chose me. Even when it cost you everything."

Elara's breath hitched. The banter, the sarcasm, the carefully maintained armor of humor—it all fell away, leaving only raw, terrifying honesty.

"I didn't choose you because it was easy, Kaelen," she whispered. "I chose you because I'm selfish. Because the thought of a world without you in it felt like death. And I know death intimately. I speak to it every day. But this—losing you—that would have been different. That would have been the kind of death I couldn't come back from."

He kissed her then. Not the desperate, frantic press of lips from before, but something slower. Deeper. A kiss that tasted of salt and ash and promises neither of them was entirely sure they could keep.

When they pulled apart, the cave was silent except for the crackling fire and their breathing—still unsteady from sharing memories that had carved them both open and left them raw.

Elara looked at Kaelen—really looked at him—and saw everything now. The boy who'd killed his cat because he was too terrified to say no. The man who'd arrested her seventeen times while wanting her every single time. The paladin who'd built walls so high he'd forgotten what it felt like to be seen.

And he was looking back at her the same way. Seeing the girl who'd been called witch-spawn and decided to wear neon-pink out of spite. The woman who spoke to the dead because the living had never listened. The necromancer who'd shown him that death wasn't the enemy—lies were.

"Elara." Her name on his lips sounded like a confession.

She closed the remaining space between them, her hand finding his jaw, fingers tracing the permanent furrow between his brows. "You don't have to keep all that distance anymore. Not with me."

"I don't know how to be close without the armor," he admitted, his voice rough.

"Then let me show you."

She kissed him, and it wasn't like the desperate kisses they'd shared before—frantic and stolen and always interrupted. This was deliberate. Claiming. A choice they were both making with full knowledge of what it meant.

Kaelen's hands came up to cradle her face, then slid into her hair, pins scattering as dark hair spilled over his fingers, the neon-pink strands threaded through it catching the light like scattered embers. "I've wanted this since the first time you called me 'darling' with that infuriating smirk."

"Seventeen arrests," Elara breathed against his mouth. "You had seventeen chances to—"

He kissed her harder, swallowing whatever she'd been about to say. His hands found the laces of her corset, and she felt his fingers trembling slightly.

"Nervous, Golden Lion?" She tried for her usual teasing tone, but it came out breathless.

"Terrified," he admitted. "That I'll do this wrong. That I'll hurt you. That you'll realize—"

"Kaelen." She pulled back enough to meet his eyes. "I've seen every corner of your soul. The parts you're proud of and the parts you hate. And I'm still here. I'm still choosing you."

Something in his expression cracked open. He kissed her again, slower this time, reverent, as his hands worked the laces free. The corset fell away, and Elara shivered—not from cold, but from the way he looked at her. Like she was something holy.

"Your turn," she said, reaching for the buckles of his armor.

He helped her, piece by piece, until he stood before her in just linen and leather. She could see his scars now—the training wound on his forearm, the claw marks from void-creatures across his ribs, the rose-gold handprint she'd left over his heart when she'd saved him from the Sun-Fire.

She traced that mark with her fingers, felt his sharp intake of breath.

"Does it hurt?" she asked.

"No." His hand covered hers, pressing her palm flat against his chest where his heart hammered. "It reminds me I'm alive. That you're real."

Elara rose on her toes, kissing the scar on his shoulder, the one at his collarbone, the faint line along his jaw. "You're real too. Not the Golden Lion. Not the Order's weapon. Just Kaelen."

"Just Kaelen," he repeated, like he was testing the words. Then his mouth found the curve of her neck, teeth grazing the sensitive spot where her pulse hammered. "Is this okay?"

"More than okay," she gasped as his hands slid down her sides, fingertips tracing the curve of her waist, her hips. "You can—Kaelen, you can touch me."

"I am touching you."

"More. I need—"

He understood. His calloused palms found bare skin beneath her skirts, and Elara's breath caught. Through the soul-tether, she felt his wonder, his desire, his absolute certainty that this was right even though everything else had been falling apart.

"Tell me if I—"

"Don't you dare stop," she commanded, and felt his smile against her throat.

They sank down together onto the bedroll, a tangle of limbs and whispered names and the silver tether between them pulsing brighter with every heartbeat. Elara had never understood why people called it "making love"—it had always seemed like such a euphemism.

But now, with Kaelen's hands mapping her body like she was territory he was desperate to know, with her own fingers threading through his hair as he kissed his way down her sternum, with the soul-bond opening completely between them so she felt every ounce of his devotion, his hunger, his overwhelming tenderness—

Now she understood.

This wasn't just physical. It was communion. Two people who'd spent their whole lives alone finally, finally letting someone in.

When they came together, the rose-gold light of their combined magic blazed through the cave. She felt everything he felt—the way she fit against him perfectly, the overwhelming rightness of it, the moment he stopped thinking and just surrendered to sensation.

And he felt everything she felt—the way she'd wanted this longer than she'd admitted, the way his careful reverence undid her more than passion would have, the absolute trust it took to let someone see her this vulnerable.

They moved together like the bond had been waiting for this all along, each touch amplified through the tether until Elara couldn't tell where her pleasure ended and his began. His name fell from her lips like a prayer. Her name sounded like salvation in his rough voice.

When they finally shattered, it was together, completely, the rose-gold light consuming them both.

Afterward, they lay tangled together, hearts still racing, the tether between them humming with contentment.

"So," Elara said eventually, trailing her fingers through the damp hair at his temple. "Was that worth eighteen years of celibate paladin training?"

Kaelen laughed—a real, unguarded sound that made her chest tight. "You're assuming I was celibate."

"You weren't?"

"I was." He pressed a kiss to her shoulder. "The Order strongly discouraged… entanglements. Said they made us weak. Made us vulnerable."

"And now?"

He propped himself up on one elbow, looking down at her with an expression so open it made her breath catch. "Now I think they were terrified of us discovering that letting someone in doesn't make you weak. It makes you brave enough to fight for something worth protecting."

Elara pulled him down for a kiss that was softer than before. Sweeter. "For someone who spent eighteen years not doing this, you're surprisingly good at it."

"I had motivation."

"Oh?"

"Seventeen arrests' worth of pent-up sexual tension is highly motivating."

She smacked his shoulder, laughing. "You arrested me because you wanted to sleep with me? That's the worst pickup strategy I've ever heard."

"I arrested you because it was the only way I was allowed to be close to you." His expression sobered. "And every single time, I hated bringing you back to that cell. Hated watching them lock you up. Hated that the only version of 'us' the world allowed was enemy and captor."

"We're not enemies anymore."

"No." He kissed her forehead, her nose, her lips. "We're not."

Through the tether, Elara felt his peace. His certainty. His absolute conviction that no matter what happened next—Order, void-rifts, High Priest—they would face it together.

She pulled him closer and let herself believe it too.

• • •

Morning came too quickly, pale light filtering through the cave entrance and pulling Elara from sleep. She was warm—warmer than she'd been in days—and it took her a moment to realize why.

Kaelen.

He was still asleep, his breathing deep and even, one arm wrapped around her waist like even unconscious he was afraid she'd disappear. His face was relaxed in a way she'd never seen while he was awake, the permanent furrow between his brows smoothed out, making him look younger. Softer.

Happy.

She let herself watch him for a moment, memorizing this version of him that the world would never get to see. Then the silver tether pulsed with a gentle warning—someone was approaching.

Kaelen's eyes snapped open instantly, warrior instincts overriding everything else. But when he saw her, his expression softened.

"Morning," he said, his voice rough with sleep.

"Morning." She kissed him quickly, then started reaching for her scattered clothes. "We have company coming. I can feel it through the bond—someone nervous, moving fast."

Kaelen was already up, pulling on his breeches with practiced efficiency. "Threat?"

"No. Just..." She concentrated on the feeling. "Young. Scared. Desperate."

They were both dressed and armed by the time footsteps approached the cave entrance, and when the young messenger burst through—mud-splattered cloak, eyes wild—Elara recognized him immediately.

Jaxon. The young courier they'd sent to Oakhaven to spread word of the Order's conspiracy.

And from the look on his face, whatever news he carried was going to change everything.

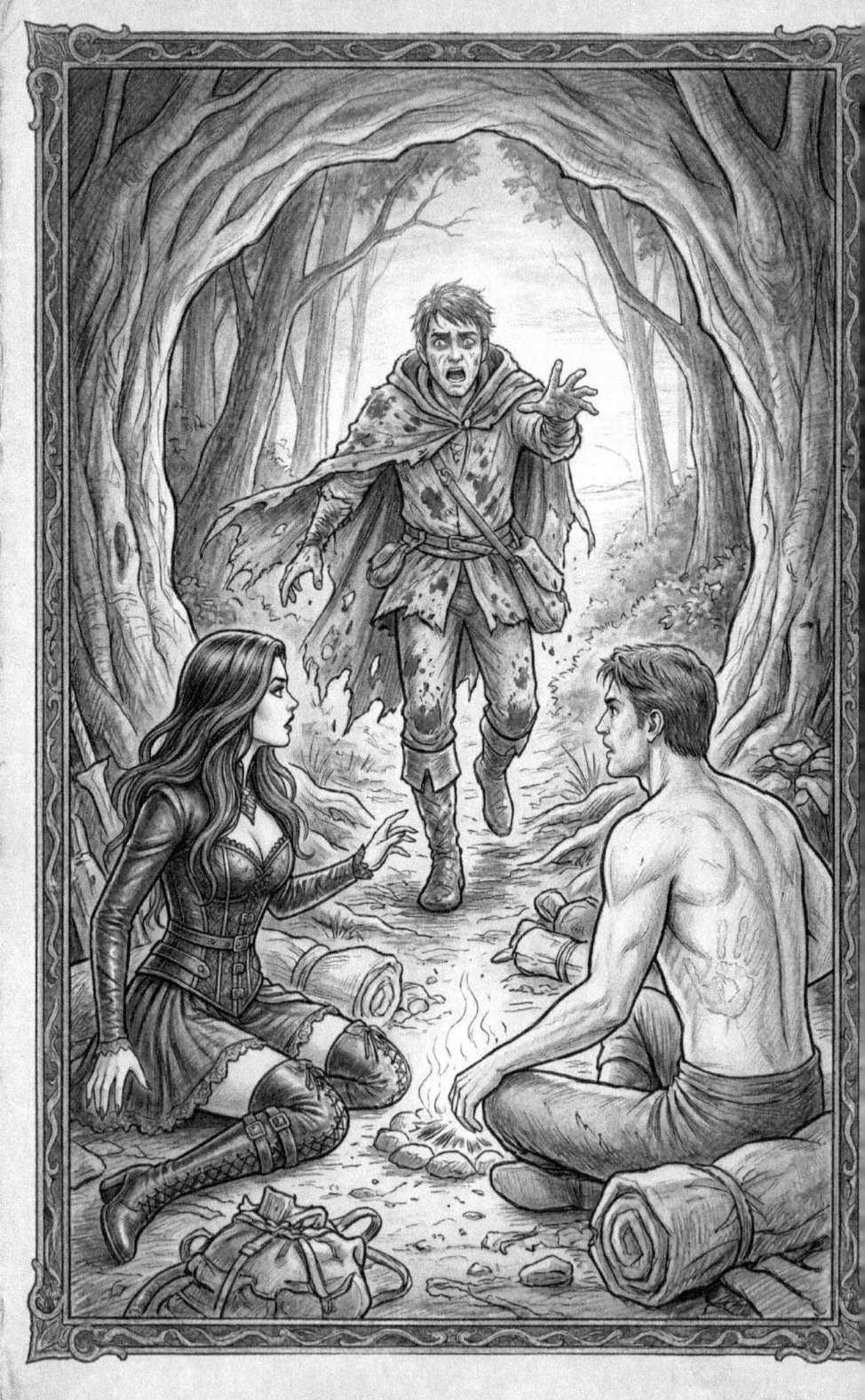

Chapter Seventeen

THE SIEGE MENTALITY

Jaxon stood at the entrance to the hollow, his chest heaving, his face flushed from what must have been hours of hard riding. His cloak was splattered with mud, and there was a fresh cut across his cheek that had only recently stopped bleeding.

But his eyes—those were what caught Elara's attention. They held the kind of exhaustion that came from witnessing something that fundamentally changed you.

"Jaxon," Kaelen said, already moving toward him, one hand extended in greeting, the other instinctively checking for threats behind the young courier. "What happened? Did you reach Oakhaven?"

"I reached it," Jaxon said, accepting Kaelen's steadying hand on his shoulder. He looked between them—at Kaelen's bare chest showing the rose-gold handprint scar, at Elara's hastily-laced dress, at the obvious intimacy of the small hollow—and had the grace to look away. "I... should I come back later?"

"No," Elara said, finishing the last of her laces with practiced efficiency. "Whatever you rode through the night to tell us, it won't wait for propriety. Sit. Catch your breath. Then talk."

Jaxon sank down onto a fallen log, gratefully accepting the water skin Kaelen offered. He drank deeply, then wiped his mouth with the back of his hand.

"I spread the word," he said, his voice hoarse. "Like you asked. I started with the market district—told everyone who would listen about what we found at Blackpine Keep. The mirrors. The inverted runes. Operation Solar Flare. Most people didn't believe me. Called me a liar. A heretic. A fool who'd been corrupted by a necromancer's lies."

Through the bond, Elara felt Kaelen's guilt spike, sharp and immediate.

"But some did," Jaxon continued, his eyes brightening slightly. "The families who'd lost people to the 'Cleansings.' The merchants who'd seen their trade routes destroyed by convenient Void-Rift appearances. The farmers whose land had been seized for 'purification.' They listened. And they started asking questions."

"How many?" Kaelen asked.

"Maybe fifty at first. Then a hundred. By the time I left three days ago..." Jaxon's voice cracked. "There were nearly five hundred people gathered in the lower city, demanding answers from the Cathedral. They wanted to see the records. Wanted to know why the void-rifts only appeared in areas the Order wanted to control. Wanted to know why the High Priest's wealth kept growing while the borderlands burned."

Elara felt a fierce surge of pride. Five hundred people. Five hundred voices demanding truth.

"What did the Order do?" she asked, though she already knew the answer would be bad. It was always bad with institutions that built their power on lies.

Jaxon's hands clenched into fists. "They called it a 'mass hysteria event.' Said the people had been poisoned by heretical propaganda.

And then..." He stopped, swallowing hard. "Then they sent the Purifiers."

The temperature in the hollow seemed to drop.

"How many dead?" Kaelen's voice was flat, emotionless—the tone he used when he was fighting to keep his emotions under control.

"Thirty-seven," Jaxon whispered. "They arrested over two hundred more. The rest scattered. I only escaped because I..." He touched the cut on his cheek. "Because one of the Purifiers recognized me. Called me by name. Said I was 'corrupted by association with the fallen Golden Lion' and that I should be cleansed."

"Who?" Kaelen asked, his voice dropping to something dangerous.

"Sir Matthias. Your friend. The one who used to spar with you in the training yard."

Through the tether, Elara felt Kaelen's grief crash over him like a wave. Matthias. Who had stood beside him for twelve years. Who had saved his life twice in the borderlands. Who had laughed at his terrible jokes and covered for him when he'd snuck extra rations to refugees.

Matthias, who had just tried to kill a boy for spreading the truth.

"I'm sorry," Jaxon said, seeing the pain in Kaelen's expression. "I know he was your brother."

"He made his choice," Kaelen said quietly. "We all did."

Elara moved to stand beside him, her hand finding his, their fingers interlacing automatically. Through the bond, she sent comfort, support, and a fierce reminder: You're not alone anymore.

"The people who escaped," Elara said, focusing back on Jaxon. "Where did they go?"

"Underground. Literally." A ghost of a smile crossed Jaxon's face. "There's a network of old smuggling tunnels beneath the lower city. The Order doesn't know about them—or at least, they pretend not to. The resistance is using them to organize. They're calling themselves the Unchained."

"The Unchained," Elara repeated, tasting the words. "I like it."

"They want to help," Jaxon continued, straightening slightly. "When I told them you were still alive, that you were planning to expose the High Priest, they..." He stopped, his voice thick with emotion. "They said they'd been waiting for someone like you. Someone who'd actually fight back instead of just accepting the Order's version of truth."

Kaelen was quiet for a long moment, processing. Five hundred people had listened to Jaxon's warning. Thirty-seven had died for demanding answers. Two hundred were in the Cathedral's dungeons, probably being "purified" even now.

And it was his fault. He'd sent Jaxon to spread the word, knowing it would paint a target on anyone who listened.

"Kaelen," Elara said softly, feeling his spiral through the bond. "Stop."

"They died because—"

"They died because the Order is corrupt and violent and terrified of the truth," she interrupted firmly. "They died because the High Priest would rather murder his own people than admit he's been lying. You didn't kill them. Valerius did."

"She's right," Jaxon said, and there was steel in his voice now. "Those people knew the risk. They chose to stand up anyway. They chose truth over safety. You can't take that choice away from them by claiming responsibility for what happened after."

Kaelen looked at the young courier—at this boy who'd lost his family to the void-rifts, who'd been used as an unwitting weapon by

THE NECROMANCER & THE GOLDEN KNIGHT

the Order, who'd ridden for three days to bring them this news despite the danger.

"Thank you," Kaelen said simply. "For everything you've risked. For believing us when you had every reason not to."

Jaxon's eyes shone with unshed tears. "You showed me the truth, sir. You could have let me keep carrying those messages, keep spreading poison without knowing. But you told me. Even though it put you in danger. Even though you were already running for your lives."

He stood, squaring his shoulders. "That's why I'm going back."

"What?" Elara and Kaelen spoke simultaneously.

"I'm going back to Oakhaven," Jaxon said, his voice steady despite the fear Elara could see in his eyes. "The Unchained need someone who knows the truth. Who saw the evidence. Who can keep organizing while you..." He gestured at them. "While you do whatever it is you're planning to do."

"Jaxon, they'll kill you," Kaelen said bluntly. "If the Purifiers catch you—"

"Then I'll die telling the truth instead of living in a lie," Jaxon interrupted. "You taught me that, sir. Both of you. You threw away everything—your position, your safety, your entire lives—because the truth mattered more than survival."

He reached into his satchel and pulled out a small, leather-bound journal. "I wrote down everything. Every detail about Blackpine Keep. The mirror fragments. The runes. The protocol documents. Even if I don't make it back, the Unchained will have the evidence."

Elara felt her throat tighten. This boy—this brave, foolish, beautiful boy—was going to get himself killed. And there was nothing she could do to stop him because he was right.

The resistance needed someone on the inside. Needed someone to keep the fire burning while they prepared their assault.

Kaelen stepped forward and pulled Jaxon into a brief, fierce embrace. "You're braver than I ever was at your age," he said quietly. "Braver than most of my brothers ever were. Your mother and sister would be proud of you."

Jaxon's composure cracked for just a moment, his face crumpling. Then something shifted in his expression—a decision being made.

"My mother," he said quietly, his voice thick with emotion. "She worked in the Cathedral for twenty years. Cleaning the High Priest's chambers. Tending his gardens. She was… faithful. Devoted. And when she became pregnant with me…" He stopped, swallowing hard. "He refused to acknowledge me. Said a child would 'complicate his divine purpose.' Paid her to disappear to the borderlands with enough coin to keep quiet."

Through the tether, Elara felt Kaelen's shock, his sudden understanding of the grey eyes, the sharp jawline, the calculated way Jaxon moved.

"You're Valerius's son," Kaelen breathed.

"Bastard son," Jaxon corrected bitterly. "The inconvenient proof that the High Priest is just a man. He sent us away when I was an infant. My mother never stopped believing in him, in the Order, in the Light. Even when the void-rift came. Even when it took her and my sister." His voice broke. "She died faithful to a man who threw us away like garbage."

"Does he know you're working against him?" Elara asked gently.

"He doesn't know anything about me," Jaxon said, a cold smile touching his lips. "I'm not real to him. Just another mess he paid to disappear. But when you march those ghosts on the Cathedral, when you expose what he's done—he'll know. He'll know his own blood chose truth over his lies."

Kaelen's grip on Jaxon's shoulder tightened. "He doesn't deserve you. Your mother didn't die for him—she died because of him. And you're going to help us make sure everyone knows it."

"I'm doing this for them," Jaxon said, his voice steady now. "So what happened to them never happens to anyone else."

"Then make sure you survive," Elara said, moving to stand beside them. "Because when we take down the Cathedral, I want you there to see it. You've earned that."

"I'll do my best." Jaxon managed a watery smile. "Though I make no promises about the survival part. I'm not exactly trained for this."

"None of us were," Kaelen said. "We're all just making it up as we go."

Jaxon laughed—a short, slightly hysterical sound. Then he sobered, looking between them one last time. "When you make your move, how will I know? How will the Unchained know when to act?"

Elara's smile was sharp and bright. "Oh, darling, you'll know. When several thousand very angry ghosts march on the Cathedral in the middle of a public execution, I think the signal will be fairly obvious."

Jaxon's eyes went wide. "Several… thousand?"

"Give or take," Elara said airily. "I haven't done a full census yet. But the Catacombs are extensive, and I'm very motivated."

"Light save us," Jaxon breathed.

"The Light had its chance," Kaelen said quietly. "Now it's our turn."

They walked Jaxon back to where he'd left his horse—a sturdy mare who looked as exhausted as her rider. As he mounted, Kaelen reached up and clasped his hand one final time.

"Jaxon," he said. "If it gets too dangerous—if the Purifiers close in—run. Don't be a hero. The resistance needs you alive, not martyred."

"I'll remember that, sir." Jaxon's grip tightened. "And Sir Kaelen? When you face Berenger… don't hesitate. I saw what men like him do when they think they're righteous. They don't stop. They don't show mercy. And they don't deserve yours."

Kaelen nodded once, the weight of that truth settling over him.

Jaxon turned his horse toward the south, toward Oakhaven and danger and the uncertain future of the Unchained resistance. But before he rode away, he looked back one last time.

"Thank you," he said simply. "For seeing me. For trusting me. For giving me something worth fighting for."

Then he was gone, swallowed by the pre-dawn darkness, leaving only the sound of hoofbeats fading into the distance.

Elara and Kaelen stood in silence for a long moment.

"He's going to die, isn't he?" Elara said quietly.

"Maybe," Kaelen admitted. "Or maybe he's going to surprise us all and live long enough to become a legend."

"I hope so," Elara said. "He deserves to see how this ends."

"So do we," Kaelen said, turning back toward the hollow where their supplies waited. "Which means we need to finish this. For him. For the thirty-seven who died. For everyone the Order has silenced."

"Then let's go raise an army," Elara said, her neon-pink eyes glowing with determination. "I hear the Grey Wastes have excellent accommodations for the vengeful dead."

Kaelen smiled despite everything. "Lead the way, necromancer."

* * *

Three Days Later

The Grey Wastes earned their name honestly.

After leaving the hollow and traveling north for three days, Elara and Kaelen stood at the edge of a landscape that looked like the world had given up. The soil wasn't brown or black—it was a flat, lifeless grey, salted so thoroughly by centuries of border wars that nothing green had grown here in living memory. Scattered across the desolate plain were the remnants of old fortifications: crumbled watchtowers, rusted siege equipment, and the occasional bleached skeleton half-buried in the ash.

It was perfect.

"Cheerful place," Elara observed, her boots crunching on the crystallized salt deposits that crusted the ground like diseased snow. "Really says 'romantic revolution planning.' Should we check for a nice spot to have a picnic?"

Kaelen, who had been scanning the horizon with the practiced eye of a military strategist, shot her a look. "This is a graveyard, Elara. The entire Northern Front was slaughtered here during the Succession Wars. There are more bodies under our feet than there were people in Oakhaven."

"I know," Elara said, her voice dropping its sarcastic edge. She closed her eyes, and even without reaching for her magic, she could feel them—thousands upon thousands of spirits, so old and so angry that they'd worn grooves into the fabric of the world itself. "I can hear them. They've been waiting a long time."

"Waiting for what?"

"Justice. Revenge. Truth. Pick your favorite." She opened her eyes, the neon-pink glow brightening in the grey twilight. "They were betrayed too, Kaelen. The proto-Order promised them glory and salvation if they fought. Instead, they got mass graves and three hundred years of silence."

Kaelen's jaw tightened. He looked down at the grey soil beneath his boots and saw not just death, but a pattern. The Order had been doing this for centuries—using people up and then burying the evidence.

"Then let's give them their voice back," he said quietly.

Elara nodded. She knelt, pressing her burned palms—still wrapped in bandages, still aching—flat against the ground. Her magic flared, sinking into the earth like roots seeking water.

"I need a general," she whispered into the grey. "Someone who remembers how to fight. Someone who died angry."

The response was immediate.

The ground in front of them didn't crack or explode. It simply… opened. Like a door swinging wide after centuries of being locked. And from that darkness, something rose.

He was massive.

Seven feet tall if he was an inch, with shoulders so broad they seemed to defy the laws of skeletal structure. He wore the remnants of armor that predated the High Order by at least two centuries— battered plate covered in a patina of rust and grave-dirt, a tattered cape of moth-eaten velvet that had once been royal blue, and a helmet crowned with the antlers of some long-extinct beast.

Where eyes should have been, there were two steady, burning points of azure light—the same cold blue as a winter sky just before a storm.

General Vane had arrived.

"Well," the specter's voice rumbled like stones grinding in a deep well, "it has been a very long time since anyone with manners asked permission before raising the dead."

Elara stood slowly, tilting her head back to meet those azure eyes. She didn't bow. She didn't flinch. She smiled—bright and sharp and absolutely delighted.

"General Vane, I presume? I'm Elara. The rude necromancer who just woke you up. This is Kaelen. The disillusioned paladin who's about to help me burn down the organization that buried you alive."

Vane's skull turned toward Kaelen, the azure lights in his sockets flickering with what might have been amusement. Or threat. It was hard to tell with a seven-foot-tall armored skeleton.

"A paladin of the Order," Vane said slowly, his voice layered with centuries of bitterness. "Come to the Wastes. Standing beside a necromancer. Either the world has ended, or the Order has finally made a mistake large enough that even their golden boys cannot ignore it."

"Both," Kaelen said, stepping forward. He didn't draw his sword—a gesture that wasn't lost on the ancient general. "The High Priest has been creating void-rifts to justify territorial expansion. They're using the same strategy your predecessors tried during the Succession Wars. Manufactured crisis. Forced salvation. Expansion under the guise of protection."

Vane was silent for a long moment. Then he laughed—a dry, rattling sound like wind through a tomb.

"I died trying to expose that exact scheme," he said, his voice dropping to something almost gentle. "My men and I refused to execute civilians in a border village. The proto-Order said the people were 'infected with shadow.' We said they were just farmers who wouldn't swear fealty. The Order buried us in the Catacombs beneath their precious Cathedral and sealed the records. We've been down there for three hundred years, boy. Watching. Waiting. Growing very, very patient."

Kaelen felt something twist in his chest—a sick recognition. The Order hadn't just failed. They'd been corrupt from the very foundation.

"We're going back to the Capital," Kaelen said, his voice steady despite the weight of the revelation. "We're going to expose the High Priest. Destroy the mirrors. Show the people what's been done in the name of the Light."

"And you want an army," Vane finished, his skeletal hand resting on the pommel of a sword that was more rust than steel. "The Border Legion. My men. The ones who died refusing to become monsters."

"Yes," Elara said simply. "We're going to wake the Catacombs. Every ancestor who was silenced. Every soldier who was buried for asking questions. Every citizen who died because they wouldn't bend the knee. We're going to give them one night to be heard."

Vane tilted his skull, considering. "That's not a revolution, girl. That's a resurrection."

"I prefer to think of it as aggressive historical revisionism," Elara replied, her smile widening. "But yes. We're going to raise the dead, storm the Cathedral, and make sure the truth comes out. Preferably while the High Priest is still alive to hear it."

"And if he fights back?" Vane asked. "If he uses the Solar Flare protocol? That weapon could level the entire city."

"Then we make sure the Ancestors act as a heat sink," Kaelen said, his tactical mind already working through the logistics. "The Catacombs run beneath the entire Capital. If Elara can anchor the spirits to the foundation stones, they can absorb and redirect the Light before it destroys everything. It won't be clean, but—"

"War never is," Vane interrupted. He looked between them—the necromancer with her neon-pink defiance and the fallen paladin with his scarred conviction—and something in his spectral form seemed to settle. "You're both going to die, you understand that? Even if we succeed, the Order won't let you walk away. They'll hunt you to the ends of the earth."

"Let them try," Elara said, her hand finding Kaelen's. The silver tether between their wrists pulsed with a steady, determined light. "We're already dead to them. Might as well make it count."

Vane's azure eyes flickered. Then he drove his sword into the grey ground with a resounding clang that echoed across the Wastes like a bell.

"The Border Legion stands with you," he declared. "Wake the Catacombs. Call the Ancestors. We've been waiting three centuries for someone brave enough—or stupid enough—to finish what we started. And necromancer?"

"Yes, General?"

"When we march, I want to be at the front. I have a few things to say to the men who buried me. And I'd prefer to say them while looking at their faces."

Elara's grin could have cut glass. "General, I think we're going to get along beautifully."

. . .

They spent the next hours planning in the ruins of an old watchtower, the three of them hunched over a map Kaelen had drawn in the dirt with a stick.

"The Catacombs have three primary access points," Kaelen explained, marking them with stones. "The main entrance through the Cathedral's lower nave—heavily guarded, sanctified ground, not an option. The old aqueduct on the eastern wall—collapsed during the last earthquake, possibly navigable for someone without a physical body."

He glanced at Vane, who nodded.

"And the third?" Elara asked.

"The mortuary tunnel," Kaelen said quietly. "It runs from the public cemetery directly into the Founders' Vault. The Order uses it to transport... remains. People who die without family. Criminals. Heretics."

"People like me," Elara observed.

"Yes."

"Perfect. I've always wanted to make a grand entrance through the trash heap."

Vane's skull turned toward her. "You find humor in strange places, necromancer."

"I find humor everywhere, General. It's called coping. You should try it. Might do wonders for your chronic death condition."

The ghost actually laughed—a real, genuine laugh that sounded like it surprised even him.

"She's right," Vane said to Kaelen. "You are going to have your hands full with this one."

"Don't I know it," Kaelen muttered, but there was warmth in his voice.

They continued planning as the grey sun set over the Grey Wastes, three figures in the dark—the necromancer, the fallen paladin, and the ghost of a general who had waited three hundred years for a second chance at justice.

By the time the stars emerged, cold and distant in the ash-choked sky, they had their plan.

"We go in tomorrow night," Kaelen said, standing and brushing the dirt from his hands. "The Order is hosting a public execution in the Cathedral Square. They're calling it a 'Cleansing Ceremony' for the souls they claim were corrupted by the void-rifts. Maximum attendance. Maximum witnesses."

"Maximum chaos when the dead start walking," Elara added with satisfaction.

Vane rose to his full, imposing height. "I'll gather the Legion. We'll be ready to march when you give the signal. And Kaelen?"

"Yes?"

"Your mentor. Berenger. He'll be there. At the Cathedral. Leading the Purifiers."

Kaelen's expression didn't change, but through the tether, Elara felt the spike of pain and rage that lanced through him.

"I know," Kaelen said quietly. "I'll handle it."

"You'll have to kill him," Vane said bluntly. "There's no middle ground with men like that. They're believers. The true kind. The kind who would rather die than admit they were wrong."

"I know," Kaelen repeated, his hand resting on the hilt of his silver sword. "I've known since the moment he tried to kill me in the ambush. He made his choice."

"And you've made yours," Elara said softly, stepping close to him. Even in the grey darkness, her pink glow was a warm, steady light.

Kaelen looked down at her—at the woman who had ruined his life and saved his soul in equal measure—and nodded.

"We're going to war," he said.

"Finally," Elara replied. "I was starting to think this revolution would never get off the ground."

Vane's azure eyes burned bright in the darkness. "Then let's make sure it's a war they never forget."

Chapter Eighteen

THE GREAT CATACOMBS

The surrender was a masterpiece of theater.

At the eastern gate of Oakhaven, just as the grey dawn broke over the city walls, Kaelen knelt in the mud with his hands raised above his head. His armor was battered, his face streaked with dirt and what the guards assumed was dried blood, and he looked every inch the broken man the Order expected.

"By the Light," one of the gate sentries breathed, his spear lowering in shock. "It's Sir Kaelen. The Golden Lion."

"Former Golden Lion," Kaelen corrected, his voice hoarse and defeated. "I've come to turn myself in. And to deliver the heretic who corrupted me."

Behind him, Elara allowed herself to be draped in iron chains that clinked dramatically as she walked. The chains were inscribed with "anti-magic" runes that would have been effective against a normal necromancer.

Elara was not normal.

She could have shattered them with a thought and a well-placed ghost. Instead, she kept her head down, her dark hair hiding her face, and played the part of the defeated witch with an enthusiasm that would have made a theater troupe weep with envy.

"The High Priest will want to see this immediately," the captain of the guard said, his eyes wide with a mix of triumph and terror. "A fallen paladin and the Necromancer. This is—this will be the trial of the century."

"I certainly hope so," Elara muttered under her breath, quiet enough that only Kaelen could hear through the tether.

They were marched through the city streets as the Capital woke. Citizens emerged from their homes, drawn by the commotion, and Elara felt the weight of their stares. Fear. Disgust. Curiosity. A few faces showed something else—sympathy, perhaps, or doubt.

Good. Doubt was a seed. And she was very good at making things grow.

The guards didn't take them to the public dungeon as expected. Instead, they were led through a series of increasingly elaborate corridors deep into the Cathedral's foundation. The air grew colder, damper, thick with the smell of old stone and older secrets.

"Where are we going?" Elara asked, injecting just the right amount of fear into her voice.

"The Pit," one of the younger guards said, his face pale. "Where they put the ones who... who need to be forgotten before the execution."

"Charming," Elara said. "Does it come with a view?"

The guard didn't answer.

They descended. And descended. The stairs were worn smooth by centuries of feet—priests, prisoners, executioners. The walls changed from carved stone to raw limestone, then to something older. The foundations of Oakhaven, laid before the High Order had even existed.

Finally, they reached a massive iron-bound door marked with the seal of the Dead—a skull wreathed in chains.

"In," the captain commanded.

Kaelen was shoved forward first. Elara followed, the chains around her wrists jangling. The door slammed shut behind them with a finality that would have been terrifying to anyone else.

The moment the guards' footsteps faded, Elara's chains began to glow neon-pink. They crumbled into rust and clattered to the stone floor.

"Well," she said, brushing the iron dust from her hands. "That was easier than expected."

"They think we're broken," Kaelen said, his defeated posture straightening back into the warrior stance he'd been born with. "They think I came crawling back to beg forgiveness and offer you up as a sacrifice."

"Did you lay it on thick enough?"

"I actually cried during the speech about how you 'poisoned my soul with your foul magics.'" Kaelen's lips quirked. "Berenger would have been proud."

Elara looked around the chamber they'd been thrown into. It wasn't a cell. It was a tomb.

No—it was the tomb. The Founders' Vault.

The walls were lined with stone sarcophagi, each one carved with names and dates that went back centuries. These were the people who had built Oakhaven before the Order had turned it into a theocracy. Merchants. Soldiers. Mothers. Fathers. People who had lived and died and expected to rest.

"They didn't rest, did they?" Elara whispered, pressing her hand against the nearest sarcophagus. "The Order sealed them down here and told the city they were being 'honored.' But really, it was about control. Silence the dead, control the past."

"Can you wake them?" Kaelen asked.

"Can I?" Elara's eyes flashed brilliant pink. "Darling, I'm going to throw them the loudest damn alarm clock in history."

She walked to the center of the vault, where a massive stone pillar held up the weight of the Cathedral's main altar directly above. The pillar was carved with hundreds of names—an honor roll of the forgotten.

Elara placed both hands on the stone. The burns on her palms had healed enough to grip, though the scars remained—a permanent reminder of the price of saving Kaelen.

"Arthur," she called softly. "I know you're here. I can feel you judging my life choices from the shadows."

A translucent shimmer materialized beside her, the ghost of Sir Arthur looking unusually somber in the oppressive atmosphere of the vault.

"This is a terrible idea, girl," Arthur said quietly. "Do you know how many spirits are down here? Thousands. Maybe tens of thousands. And they've been trapped for centuries. They're not going to wake up gentle."

"I'm counting on that," Elara replied. She looked up at the ceiling, at the massive weight of stone and lies pressing down on them. "The High Priest thinks he's won. He thinks we came here to die. So let's show him what resurrection really looks like."

She closed her eyes and reached.

Not gently. Not with the careful, respectful touch she usually used when communing with the dead. This was a summoning. A call to arms. A declaration of war written in neon-pink across the fabric of death itself.

"WAKE UP!" Her voice didn't shout—it resonated, vibrating through the stone, through the bones, through the very foundations of the city.

The response was a rumble that started deep in the earth and built like an oncoming earthquake.

The sarcophagi didn't open. The dead didn't rise as shambling corpses. Instead, they simply... stepped through.

Translucent forms began to emerge from the walls, from the floor, from the stone itself. Men in ancient armor. Women in work clothes. Children who should have lived to grow old. They came in waves, filling the vault with a spectral light that had nothing to do with the Order's harsh white glow and everything to do with memory made manifest.

And at their head, rising from a sarcophagus marked with military honors, was General Vane.

His azure eyes blazed in the darkness like twin stars.

"Well," the General said, his spectral form solidifying into something almost corporeal. "I see you made it. And you brought the party directly to the dancing hall. Efficient."

"I learned from the best," Elara said, grinning despite the exhaustion already creeping into her bones. Waking this many spirits at once was like trying to hold back a river with her bare hands.

Kaelen stepped forward, addressing the assembled dead with the commanding presence of a military leader.

"Ancestors of Oakhaven," he said, his voice ringing clear. "The High Order has lied to you. They've lied to your children. They've lied to this entire city. Tomorrow night, they plan to execute more civilians in the Cathedral Square, claiming the deaths are necessary to 'purge the shadow.' But the shadow is their own creation. The void-rifts are weapons. The Solar Flare is mass murder. And the only thing standing between truth and annihilation is us."

The spirits murmured—a sound like wind through a canyon.

"We need you to hold the foundations," Kaelen continued. "When we reveal the truth, the High Priest will try to use the Solar

Flare to destroy the evidence and everyone in it. We need you to absorb that energy. Redirect it. Save the city your labor built."

"And in exchange?" a woman's ghost asked, her form flickering. "What do the living offer the dead?"

"The truth," Elara said simply. "Your stories. Your names. Your lives given back to the people who forgot you. No more silence. No more being used as props for the Order's theater. You get to be heard. One last time."

The vault went silent.

Then, slowly, the spirits began to kneel. Not in supplication, but in acceptance. In solidarity.

"The Founders stand with you," the woman said. "Wake the deeper sleepers. Wake the Border Legion. Wake every soul that died questioning the Light. It's time the Cathedral learned what happens when the dead stop being polite."

Vane's spectral form blazed brighter. "My Legion is ready. We've been ready for three hundred years. Just give us the signal."

Elara looked at Kaelen. Through the tether, she felt his determination, his rage, and underneath it all, his bone-deep love for a city that had been twisted into something monstrous.

"Tomorrow night," Kaelen said. "During the Cleansing Ceremony. We let them gather. We let them feel safe in their lies. And then—"

"We flip the table," Elara finished, her smile sharp and bright. "And we make sure everyone sees what falls out."

The dead roared their approval—a sound that shook dust from the ancient stones and made the iron door rattle in its frame.

Above them, in the Cathedral, the priests continued their preparations for the execution, blissfully unaware that beneath their feet, an army of the forgotten was preparing to remind them that history never stays buried forever.

Chapter Nineteen

CALLING THE ANCESTORS

The Cathedral Square was packed.

Citizens filled every available space—the steps, the archways, even the rooftops of neighboring buildings. They had come for the spectacle, for the "Cleansing Ceremony" the High Order had been advertising for days. Banners hung from the Cathedral spires, each one emblazoned with the sun-sigil and promises of "purification" and "salvation."

At the center of the square stood the pyre.

It was a massive construction of blessed oak and sanctified iron, designed to burn hot enough to reduce a human body to ash in minutes. The Order called it the "Light's Mercy." Everyone else called it what it was: a public execution dressed up in prayer.

High Priest Valerius stood on the Cathedral's grand balcony, his white robes gleaming in the artificial glow of the solar mirrors positioned above the square. He looked like a figure from a religious painting—serene, confident, absolutely certain of his righteousness.

"Citizens of Oakhaven," his voice rang out, magically amplified to reach every corner of the square. "Tonight, we cleanse the corruption that has taken root in our beloved city. The void-rifts were born from dark magic—from necromancy—from those who traffic with death instead of embracing the Light. Tonight, we burn the source of the plague. Tonight, we are saved."

The crowd murmured. Some cheered. Others looked uncomfortable, their faces tight with doubt.

Good, Elara thought from her position deep beneath the Cathedral, in the darkness of the Catacombs. Doubt was her friend tonight.

She stood at the base of the great pillar, her hands pressed against the stone, her magic already flowing into the foundations like water finding cracks. Around her, the spirits of the Catacombs waited—thousands of them, patient and ready.

Kaelen stood beside her, one hand on her shoulder, the other on his sword. Through the tether, she could feel his controlled fury, his determination, and underneath it all, his absolute trust in her.

"Are you ready?" he asked quietly.

Elara's eyes opened, glowing brilliant pink in the darkness. "I was born ready, darling. Let's show them what the dead have to say."

She took a breath and reached deeper than she'd ever reached before.

Not for individual spirits. Not for specific souls. She reached for all of them. Every ancestor buried in Oakhaven's soil. Every forgotten soldier in the Grey Wastes. Every executed heretic whose ashes had been scattered in the river. She called to the memory of the city itself—to the stones and bones and blood-soaked earth that held centuries of truth.

"RISE," she commanded, her voice echoing through the tether, through the Catacombs, through the very bedrock of the city.

The response was immediate and catastrophic.

* * *

In the Cathedral Square, the flagstones began to glow.

Not with the High Order's harsh white light, but with a soft, neon-pink luminescence that seeped up through the cracks between the stones like dawn breaking from underground.

The crowd gasped. A few people stumbled backward. The High Priest's serene expression flickered with the first hint of alarm.

"Do not be afraid," Valerius called out, his voice strained. "This is merely a test of your faith! The darkness seeks to frighten you, but the Light—"

The first ghost emerged in the middle of the pyre.

She was an old woman, her translucent form wearing the simple dress of a merchant's wife. Her eyes were kind, sad, and very, very angry. She looked around at the crowd, at the pyre that would have burned her great-great-grandchildren, and she spoke.

Her voice didn't come from her lips. It came from everywhere— from the stones, from the air, from the hearts of everyone present.

"My name was Miriam Ashford," the ghost said, her words cutting through the square like a bell. "I died fifty-three years ago of a fever. The Order told my children I was at peace. They lied. They sealed me in the Catacombs and used my bones to sanctify their wards. I was not a heretic. I was a mother. And I have been listening."

More ghosts began to rise.

A soldier in ancient armor stepped through the wall of the Cathedral itself. "I am Captain Henrik. I died three hundred years ago refusing to burn a village of farmers. The Order called me a traitor. They buried me alive. I have been waiting to finish my report."

A young woman emerged from the fountain, her form dripping with spectral water. "My name is Sarah. I was fifteen when the Order burned me for 'consorting with shadow.' My crime was reading books they didn't approve of. I remember every page."

One by one, dozens, then hundreds, then thousands of ghosts began to manifest throughout the square. They didn't attack. They didn't threaten. They simply stood and bore witness—each one a living contradiction to the Order's carefully constructed narrative.

And with each manifestation came a memory.

Not spoken, but shared. Broadcast directly into the minds of every living person in the square through the network of neon-pink magic that Elara had woven through the city's foundations.

The citizens of Oakhaven saw:

—The proto-Order burying General Vane and his men alive for refusing to commit atrocities.

—The High Priest's predecessors creating the first void-rift as a "controlled demonstration" of divine power.

—Fifty years of systematic executions, each one disguised as necessary cleansing, each victim guilty of nothing more than asking questions.

—The mirrors. The awful, beautiful truth about the mirrors—how they focused the Light not to destroy darkness, but to create it. How every void-rift was born from the Order's own weapons.

—And finally, the Solar Flare protocol. The High Priest's plan to level the border provinces entirely, blame it on "shadow corruption," and claim the scorched earth as sanctified territory.

The silence that fell over Cathedral Square was absolute.

Then someone screamed.

Not in terror. In rage.

"You lied!" a man in the crowd shouted, his face twisted with betrayal. "My brother died in the borderlands! You said he was a hero! You said he died fighting the Void!"

"My daughter," a woman cried, her voice breaking. "You burned my daughter! She was seven years old! You said she was corrupted!"

The crowd surged—not toward the pyre, but toward the Cathedral steps, where the Purifiers stood in their blessed armor, suddenly looking very small and very vulnerable.

On the balcony, High Priest Valerius's serene mask finally cracked.

"SILENCE!" he roared, his hands beginning to glow with that terrible, artificial white light. "You are being deceived by dark magic! The witch in the Catacombs is twisting your minds! This is the corruption I warned you about!"

"The only corruption here," a new voice rang out, "is yours."

Kaelen stepped out onto the Cathedral's front steps.

He wasn't wearing his golden armor. He was dressed in simple leathers, his sword bare silver at his side. The handprint scar on his ribs was visible through his open shirt—a permanent testament to the price of truth.

"My name is Kaelen," he said, his voice amplified not by magic but by the perfect acoustics of the square and the absolute silence of the crowd. "I was the Golden Lion. I arrested necromancers. I hunted heretics. I believed every lie the Order told me because I thought the Light was pure."

He looked up at the High Priest, his eyes hard as flint.

"But the Light isn't pure. It's a weapon. And the darkness you claim to fight? You created it. You've been creating it for three hundred years. And I'm done being your sword."

The crowd erupted in chaos—some shouting support, others demanding explanations, still others simply weeping as the weight of centuries of lies crashed down on them.

Valerius raised his hands, the solar mirrors above the Cathedral beginning to hum with gathering energy.

"If you will not be saved," the High Priest said, his voice cold and absolute, "then you will be purged."

The mirrors tilted, catching the dying sunlight and magnifying it into a pillar of concentrated, destructive power.

The Solar Flare was charging.

· · ·

In the Catacombs, Elara felt the massive surge of energy building above her.

"Now, General!" she screamed.

Vane and the Border Legion surged upward through the stone, their spectral forms blazing with azure light. They didn't attack the Purifiers—not yet. Instead, they spread throughout the Cathedral's foundation, each ghost placing themselves at a crucial structural point.

When the Solar Flare discharged, it didn't explode outward.

The ghosts absorbed it.

Thousands of spectral forms acting as a heat sink, pulling the destructive energy into themselves and redirecting it harmlessly into the earth. The Cathedral shook. Windows shattered. Stone cracked.

But the square—the people—survived.

Valerius stared in horror as his ultimate weapon sputtered and died, consumed by the very dead he had tried to silence.

"Impossible," he whispered.

"Not impossible," Elara said, stepping out of the Cathedral's main doors to stand beside Kaelen. Her dark hair was wild, the pink strands blazing bright as her eyes glowed with power, and she looked every inch the monster the Order had always claimed she was. "Just inconvenient. For you."

She raised her hand, and every ghost in Oakhaven turned to look at the High Priest.

"Your move," she said sweetly.

Chapter Twenty

THE BATTLE OF THE CATHEDRAL

The High Priest did not go quietly.

"PURIFIERS!" Valerius's voice cracked across the square like a whip. "Defensive formation! Deploy the Sun-Fire ordnance! Kill the traitor and burn the witch!"

The elite knights of the Order moved with practiced precision, forming a shield wall on the Cathedral steps. Their armor blazed with channeled Light, and in their hands, blessed spears began to glow with that same crystalline white fire that had nearly killed Kaelen.

But they weren't facing mortals anymore.

General Vane rose through the stone steps like a leviathan breaching the surface of the ocean. His spectral form towered over the Purifiers, seven feet of ancient fury wrapped in rust and vengeance.

"BORDER LEGION!" His voice rolled across the square like thunder. "ADVANCE!"

From every shadow, every alley, every crack in the cobblestones, the ghosts came.

These weren't the gentle spirits of grandmothers and merchants. These were soldiers—men and women who had died in battle, who remembered the weight of steel and the taste of blood. They carried spectral weapons that gleamed with azure light, and when they clashed with the Purifiers, the sound was like a thousand bells ringing in discord.

The Battle of the Cathedral had begun.

*   *   *

Kaelen didn't wait for orders. He drew his silver sword and charged directly into the center of the Purifier line.

The first knight swung at him with a blessed mace that would have shattered his skull. Kaelen ducked, drove his shoulder into the man's midsection, and used his momentum to flip him over the shield wall. Before the Purifier could recover, a spectral soldier from the Border Legion was on him, pinning him to the ground.

"Non-lethal if possible!" Kaelen shouted to the ghosts. "These are my brothers! They've been lied to the same as I was!"

"They're trying to kill us!" a ghost shot back, parrying a spear thrust.

"Then disarm them! Break their weapons! But give them a chance to surrender!"

It was chaos. Beautiful, terrible chaos.

Elara stood at the top of the Cathedral steps, her hands raised, conducting the battle like a maestro leading an orchestra. She didn't fight directly—she couldn't, not without exhausting herself completely. Instead, she coordinated.

A Purifier broke through the ghost line, charging toward a group of civilians. Elara flicked her wrist, and a spectral wall of ancient builders rose between them, their translucent forms interlocking into an impenetrable barrier.

Three knights tried to flank Kaelen. Elara whispered a command, and Sir Arthur materialized behind them, his translucent form flickering into something horrifying—mouth stretched too wide, eyes hollow and vast, his entire being radiating the theatrical terror he'd spent two hundred years perfecting.

The Purifiers screamed and scattered.

"I'm helping!" Arthur called cheerfully, resuming his normal pompous appearance.

"You're terrifying!" Elara called back.

"I contain multitudes!"

Across the square, General Vane was a force of nature. He didn't just fight the Purifiers—he dismantled them. A sweep of his spectral blade shattered a shield. A gesture from his hand sent a wave of ghostly soldiers crashing over a defensive position like a tsunami.

But he never killed. He'd spent three centuries thinking about this moment, and he'd decided long ago that he wouldn't become the monster the Order had accused him of being.

"YIELD!" he roared at a Purifier commander who was desperately trying to rally his men. "You're fighting for a lie! Lay down your weapons!"

"Never!" the commander shouted back, raising his blessed spear. "The Light demands—"

Vane's massive spectral hand closed around the spear and crushed it to powder.

"The Light," Vane said quietly, "demands nothing. It's just light. You're the one who decided to turn it into a weapon. Now drop the steel before I make you."

The commander looked at his ruined weapon, then at the army of the dead surrounding him, then at the High Priest on the balcony—who was notably not coming to his aid.

He dropped the broken spear.

"Stand down," he said to his men, his voice hollow. "It's over."

· · ·

But it wasn't over. Not yet.

On the balcony, High Priest Valerius watched his carefully constructed empire crumble. The Purifiers were surrendering. The citizens were turning against him. The dead were testifying. And worst of all, his perfect weapon—the Solar Flare—had been neutralized by the very corpses he'd tried to silence.

He wouldn't allow it.

The High Priest turned and strode back into the Cathedral's inner sanctum, his white robes billowing behind him. He had one final card to play. One last mirror that the rebels didn't know about.

The Prime Lens.

Hidden in the Cathedral's highest tower, it was the original mirror—the first one the Order's founders had created when they discovered how to weaponize the Light. It was smaller than the others, but infinitely more concentrated. More dangerous.

Valerius climbed the tower stairs three at a time, his breath coming in ragged gasps. He was old—older than anyone knew, sustained by life-force stolen from the borderlands through the void-rifts.

But even gods could fall. And he would fall standing, burning the world with him if necessary.

He reached the tower apex and placed his hands on the Prime Lens.

"By the authority vested in me by the Unconquered Sun," he began, channeling every ounce of power he had left, "I declare this city—"

"No."

Valerius froze.

Standing in the doorway was a young man with familiar grey eyes and a sharp jawline that mirrored his own. Jaxon. The bastard son he'd paid to disappear twenty years ago. The inconvenient proof that the High Priest was just a man.

"Jaxon," Valerius said carefully, his hands still on the mirror. "What are you doing here? You should have fled the city when—"

"When you sent the Purifiers to kill me?" Jaxon interrupted, his voice steady despite the tremor Elara would have felt if she'd been close enough. "When you let mother and my sister burn in a void-rift you created? When you made me spread your poisoned lies for six months without telling me what I was carrying?"

Valerius's face remained impassive. "I gave your mother enough coin to live comfortably. What she chose to do with it—where she chose to settle—was not my concern."

"She loved you," Jaxon said, and now his voice cracked. "Even at the end, when the rift was consuming her, she prayed to the Light. She prayed for you. She died faithful to a man who never once acknowledged her existence."

"Sentiment," Valerius dismissed. "Your mother understood the necessity of discretion. A High Priest cannot be seen to have... earthly entanglements. It would undermine the divine authority of the office."

"I'm not an entanglement," Jaxon said, his hand moving to the hilt of his short sword. "I'm your son."

"You are a mistake I corrected," Valerius said coldly. "And if you've come here seeking some sentimental reconciliation, some moment of paternal recognition, you will be disappointed. I have more important concerns than the bastard offspring of a servant."

Jaxon's laugh was bitter. "I don't want your recognition. I want you to stop."

"Stop?" Valerius's hand tightened on the Prime Lens. "Stop saving this world from itself? Stop providing order to chaos? Stop giving purpose to the masses who would flounder without divine guidance?"

"Stop killing people!" Jaxon shouted, his composure finally breaking. "Stop creating the very darkness you claim to fight! Stop lying!"

Valerius's expression hardened. "Then you're a traitor too. Just like your mother—weak, sentimental, unable to see the necessary sacrifices that progress demands."

He triggered the Prime Lens.

The beam of Light that erupted wasn't aimed at the city. It was aimed at Jaxon.

* * *

In the square below, Elara felt the surge of power and looked up.

"Kaelen!" she screamed. "The tower!"

Kaelen didn't hesitate. He grabbed a fallen Purifier's shield and sprinted for the Cathedral doors, ghosts clearing a path ahead of him.

He burst into the tower stairwell just in time to see Jaxon fly backward from the force of the Light blast, his body hitting the stone wall with a sickening crack.

"NO!" Kaelen roared.

He threw the shield like a discus. It caught the edge of the Prime Lens, knocking it off-axis. The beam of Light careened wildly, striking the tower's ceiling and causing stone to rain down.

Valerius turned, his eyes wild. "You! You ruined everything! My perfect system! My perfect Light!"

"Your system was rotten from the foundation," Kaelen said, his sword in his hand as he climbed the last few steps. "And I'm here to tear it down."

They faced each other in the tower—the fallen paladin and the corrupt priest, with Jaxon's barely breathing form between them.

"You can't win," Valerius said, his hands beginning to glow again. "Even if you kill me, the Order survives. The Light survives. It's bigger than one man."

"You're right," Kaelen agreed. "It is bigger than one man. That's why I'm not fighting alone."

Behind him, the stairwell filled with neon-pink light.

Elara emerged, flanked by General Vane and a dozen spectral soldiers. Her eyes were blazing, the pink streaks in her dark hair crackling with barely contained power.

"Step away from the lens," she commanded. "And step away from that boy. Your son deserves better than to die at his father's hands."

Valerius's gaze flicked to Jaxon's crumpled form, and for a moment—just a moment—something that might have been emotion crossed his face. Then it was gone, replaced by cold calculation.

"He was never my son," Valerius said. "Just another tool. Another sacrifice necessary for the greater good."

"Then you're already dead," Elara said quietly. "Because a man who can't recognize his own blood isn't human anymore. He's just a hollow thing wearing a priest's robes."

Valerius looked at them—at the coalition of the living and the dead, at the truth he could no longer suppress, at the son who had chosen justice over the father who had abandoned him.

And he made his choice.

He lunged for the Prime Lens, channeling a desperate surge of stolen life-force. Not to overload it—to weaponize it one final time.

The beam that erupted was wild, uncontrolled. It struck General Vane's spectral form, dispersing the ghost momentarily. The Lens cracked under the strain, fractures spider-webbing across its surface.

Valerius grabbed the fragmenting mirror, not caring as the edges cut his palms, and ran.

"Stop him!" Elara shouted, but Kaelen was already moving—not toward Valerius, but toward Jaxon.

The young man was dying. The Light-burn from the initial blast was spreading through his chest, the same crystalline poison that had nearly killed Kaelen weeks ago.

Kaelen had a choice: pursue the High Priest, or save the boy.

He chose the boy.

"Elara!" he called, dropping to his knees beside Jaxon. "I need you!"

Elara's magic flared as she rushed to them, her hands already glowing pink. Through the tether, Kaelen felt her understanding, her approval of his choice. People over vengeance. Always.

Behind them, Valerius disappeared through a hidden passage, his white robes vanishing into the darkness of the Cathedral's depths. His voice echoed back, raw with fury and pain:

"This isn't over! The Light will purge you all!"

Then he was gone.

Vane's spectral form reformed, crackling with barely contained rage. "He's fleeing to the inner sanctum. The heart of the Cathedral. If he reaches the Founders' Mirror—"

"Later," Kaelen said firmly, his hands supporting Jaxon's head. "First, we save him."

Jaxon's eyes flickered open, meeting Kaelen's gaze. Grey eyes so like his father's, but filled with something Valerius had never possessed—humanity.

"You… let him go," Jaxon whispered, disbelief in his voice. "For me."

"You're worth more than revenge," Kaelen said simply. "Now hold still. This is going to hurt."

Elara's magic poured into the wound, violet-dark and powerful, pulling the Light-poison out with the same technique she'd used on Kaelen. Jaxon screamed, his back arching, but Kaelen held him steady.

When it was done, when the last of the crystalline infection had been drawn out and dissolved, Jaxon lay gasping but alive. The wound on his chest was scarred, but clean.

"He'll live," Elara said, exhaustion heavy in her voice. "But he needs rest. Real rest. Days of it."

Kaelen looked toward the passage where Valerius had fled, then back at Jaxon. The boy—the man—who had confronted his father and survived.

Kaelen rushed to Jaxon's side, checking for a pulse. "He's alive. Barely."

Elara knelt beside them, her magic already flowing into the young man's wounds. "I can stabilize him. But we need to get him out of here. This tower's not stable."

As if to punctuate her point, the ceiling groaned ominously.

They fled—Kaelen carrying Jaxon, Elara and Vane guarding their retreat—as the tower began to collapse behind them. The Prime Lens shattered, its fragments raining down into the Cathedral below like deadly snow.

When they emerged into the square, the battle was over.

The Purifiers had surrendered. The citizens were helping the wounded. And the ghosts—thousands of them—stood peacefully among the living, bearing witness to the dawn of something new.

When they emerged into the square, the battle was over.

The Purifiers had surrendered. The citizens were helping the wounded. And the ghosts—thousands of them—stood peacefully among the living, bearing witness to the dawn of something new.

General Vane materialized beside them, his azure eyes blazing with urgency.

"The High Priest has barricaded himself in the inner sanctum," the ghost reported. "He's wounded, desperate, and he still has access to the Founders' Mirror—the most ancient and powerful lens in the Cathedral. If he manages to weaponize it—"

"Then we stop him," Kaelen said, looking down at Jaxon. The young man was stable now, breathing easier, the worst of the poison drawn out. "But not yet. Not until we know Jaxon is safe."

"Sir Kaelen," Jaxon said, his voice weak but insistent. "Don't wait for me. He'll destroy everything if you give him time. Go. Finish it."

Kaelen hesitated, torn between protecting the boy he'd saved and stopping the monster who'd created all this suffering.

Elara's hand found his. Through the tether, he felt her certainty, her strength.

"The Unchained are here," she said, gesturing to where members of the resistance were emerging from the smuggling tunnels, rushing to help the wounded. "They'll care for him. But Valerius won't wait. He's cornered, and cornered things are most dangerous."

Kaelen looked around at the destruction, at the truth finally laid bare, at the city that would never be the same. The High Priest was still alive, still dangerous, still capable of one final atrocity.

"We finish this," he said quietly, standing. He looked down at Jaxon one last time. "You were braver than he ever deserved. Rest now. When you wake up, your father will answer for everything he's done."

Jaxon nodded, tears streaming down his face—not of grief, but of relief and exhaustion and the beginning of healing.

As resistance members carefully lifted him, Kaelen turned toward the Cathedral entrance where Elara waited, her neon-pink glow steady in the pre-dawn darkness.

"Together?" she asked, offering her hand.

"Always," he replied, taking it.

The sun was beginning to rise over Oakhaven, but their work wasn't done.

The High Priest was still alive. And he had one final weapon to use.

Chapter Twenty-One

THE DUEL

The Great Hall of the Cathedral was a skeletal ruin of its former glory.

Liquid silver from the shattered mirrors dripped from the vaulted ceiling like slow, metallic rain, hissing as it struck the cooling flagstones. The massive rose window—once a masterpiece of stained glass depicting the sun's triumph over darkness—now gaped open to the night sky, its fragments scattered across the floor in a thousand glittering pieces.

Kaelen dropped from the upper gallery, his boots hitting stone with a crack that echoed through the empty space. His sword was drawn, his breathing controlled, but his heart was hammering against his ribs with a rhythm that had nothing to do with exertion and everything to do with what he knew was coming.

He'd felt Berenger's presence the moment he'd entered the Cathedral. Through years of training together, of fighting side-by-side, of sharing the weight of the Order's demands, they'd developed an awareness of each other that went beyond the physical.

His mentor was here. And one of them wasn't leaving alive.

The heavy, rhythmic clanking of plate armor echoed from the shadows near the high altar. Sir Berenger stepped into the moonlight filtering through the broken window. He had discarded his ceremonial shield—a telling choice. In his hands, he gripped a massive two-handed claymore that hummed with a desperate, overcharged radiance.

The sword was burning him. Kaelen could see it—the way Berenger's gauntlets smoked where they gripped the blessed steel, the way his movements were slightly too stiff, as if the Light he channeled was eating him from within.

He was using forbidden techniques. Drawing on more power than any mortal body could safely contain. This wasn't a duel he intended to walk away from.

"You look tired, Kaelen," Berenger said, his voice echoing hollowly inside his helm. The warm, gruff tone Kaelen remembered from his training days was gone, replaced by something flat and cold. "That's the problem with icons. Once they tarnish, they're just scrap metal."

"I'm not an icon, Berenger," Kaelen replied, his silver sword catching the moonlight. "And I'm done being your masterpiece."

"You were never mine," Berenger said, and for a moment—just a moment—there was something that sounded like regret in his voice. "You were the Order's. From the moment your father died and left you on our doorstep, you belonged to something greater than yourself. I just helped shape you."

"You helped break me," Kaelen corrected. "You stood there and watched while they made me kill my cat. You taught me that love was weakness and mercy was failure. You turned me into a weapon."

"I made you into a Lion!" Berenger roared, his control fracturing. "I gave you purpose! Strength! A legacy that would have outlived us both! And you threw it away for a witch who traffics with corpses!"

He lunged.

The weight of the claymore should have made him slow, but Berenger moved with the frantic, desperate speed of a man who knew he was already dead and just wanted to take his failure with him. The blade came down in a massive, vertical arc designed to split Kaelen from crown to sternum.

Kaelen sidestepped, his smaller sword coming up to deflect rather than block. The impact still sent a jar of white-hot pain up his arms, but he used the momentum, spinning away and creating distance.

"I didn't throw it away," Kaelen said, his voice steady despite the adrenaline flooding his system. "I woke up. There's a difference."

They circled each other in the ruined hall, two figures moving through the silver rain like dancers in a nightmare ballet.

"The Order gave you everything," Berenger insisted, his sword leaving trails of light in the air as he pressed forward with a series of brutal, horizontal slashes. "Without us, you would have been nothing. An orphan. A beggar. We made you matter."

Kaelen parried, ducked, retreated. He wasn't trying to kill Berenger—not yet. Some part of him, the part that still remembered sitting beside this man in the mess hall, learning how to properly care for a blade, listening to stories about battles won and brothers lost— that part still hoped there was a way out that didn't end in blood.

"You made me a slave," Kaelen said, catching Berenger's blade in a bind and twisting, trying to disarm him. "You made me believe that being broken was the same as being strong. That sacrificing my humanity was holy. That killing innocents was justified if we called it 'purification.'"

Berenger wrenched his sword free, staggering back. The Light around his blade flickered—his strength was failing, the forbidden technique eating through his reserves.

"They weren't innocents!" he shouted, and now there was desperation in his voice. "They were infected! Corrupted! The void-rifts—"

"Were created by us!" Kaelen interrupted, his sword leveling at Berenger's chest. "You know it. You've always known it. I saw the records, Berenger. I saw the experiments. The proto-Order discovered that focused Light could fracture reality. They've been creating the Void for three hundred years to justify expansion. And you helped them."

"I followed orders!" Berenger's voice cracked. "I did my duty!"

"So did the men who buried General Vane alive," Kaelen said quietly. "So did every soldier who ever committed an atrocity and claimed they were 'just following orders.' It doesn't absolve you. It just makes you a coward."

The word hit Berenger like a physical blow.

For a moment, the older knight stood perfectly still, his sword trembling in his hands. Then, with a roar that was half-rage and half-despair, he charged.

This time, Kaelen didn't retreat.

He met Berenger head-on, his silver blade moving in the forms they had practiced together a thousand times. Parry, riposte, sidestep, counter. They moved through the sequence like it was choreographed, each knowing exactly what the other would do because they had learned from the same teacher, fought in the same battles, bled for the same lies.

But Kaelen had changed. He didn't fight like a Lion anymore—rigid, powerful, overwhelming. He fought like a man who had learned that survival sometimes meant bending. He used the environment—ducking behind a fallen pillar, using the slick silver on the floor to throw off Berenger's footing, exploiting every opening.

And slowly, brutally, he began to win.

A strike to Berenger's knee that made the older knight stumble. A slash across his sword arm that weakened his grip. A pommel strike to the side of his helmet that left him reeling.

"Stay down," Kaelen said, his voice rough with emotion as Berenger fell to one knee. "Please, Berenger. Just stay down. You don't have to die for them."

Berenger's helm turned up toward him, the eye slits dark and empty.

"Yes," he said quietly. "I do."

He surged upward one final time, the claymore swinging in a last, desperate arc.

Kaelen didn't have a choice anymore.

His silver sword went through the gap in Berenger's gorget, the blade punching clean through the weak point in the armor. The older knight's momentum carried him forward, and for a heartbeat, they were face-to-face, so close Kaelen could see his mentor's eyes through the visor.

There was no anger there. Just a terrible, weary relief.

"Thank you," Berenger whispered, blood bubbling at his lips. "For... for ending this."

Then the Light in his armor didn't fade—it shrieked. A final, blinding pulse of holy energy erupted from the dying knight, throwing Kaelen backward across the hall. He hit the base of the altar with enough force to crack stone, his vision swimming in white.

When his sight cleared, Berenger was gone. Not dead in the traditional sense—consumed. The forbidden technique he'd been using had burned through him completely, leaving nothing behind but an empty suit of armor and a handful of ash.

Kaelen lay there, his whole body screaming in pain, and stared at the spot where his mentor had been.

He had won. The duel was over.

So why did it feel like he'd lost something he could never get back?

"Kaelen!"

Elara was suddenly there, sliding to her knees beside him, her hands already glowing pink as she checked him for injuries. Behind her, the doorway to the hall was blocked by a shimmering wall of spectral soldiers—she'd been holding off the remaining Purifiers while he fought, giving him the space he needed.

"I'm fine," he managed, though his voice sounded hollow even to his own ears.

"You're not fine," she said, her fingers gentle as they probed the new bruises blooming across his ribs. "You just killed your father figure and got thrown across a room by a Light explosion. You're allowed to not be fine."

Kaelen looked at her—at the woman who had seen every dark corner of his soul and chosen to stay anyway—and something in his chest cracked open.

"He thanked me," he whispered. "At the end. He thanked me for killing him."

Elara's expression softened. She didn't offer platitudes or try to minimize what had happened. She just took his hand in hers, the silver tether between them pulsing with a warm, steady light.

"He was trapped," she said quietly. "By the Order. By his own beliefs. By the weight of everything he'd done in their name. You didn't just end his life, Kaelen. You freed him. Whether he deserved that freedom or not... that's not for us to judge."

"I keep thinking about Barnaby," Kaelen said, the words tumbling out before he could stop them. "My cat. The one they made me kill. And I wonder—did Berenger ever have a Barnaby? Was there a moment when someone broke him the way he helped break me? Or was he always... this?"

"I don't know," Elara admitted. "But I know this—you're not him. You broke the cycle. You chose differently. And that matters."

Kaelen pulled her close, burying his face in her hair, breathing in the scent of peonies and graveyard dirt and life. Through the tether, he felt her love for him—fierce, unconditional, utterly unshakable.

"One more," he said, his voice steadying. "The High Priest. Then it's done."

Elara's expression shifted, something dark crossing her features. "Kaelen... Valerius escaped. He's wounded, cornered in the inner sanctum. Vane says he's trying to activate the Founders' Mirror."

He pulled back, searching her face. The relief he'd felt moments ago evaporated, replaced by grim determination.

"The Founders' Mirror?" he asked.

"The original lens. The first mirror the Order ever created." Elara helped him sit up, her magic flowing into his bruised ribs. "If he activates it with his stolen life-force, he could level the entire city. Turn it all into one massive void-rift."

Kaelen absorbed this, processing. The man who had orchestrated everything—the void-rifts, the lies, the systematic murder of thousands—was making one final desperate play.

"And Jaxon?" he asked.

"Alive. Healing. The Unchained have him." Elara's eyes softened. "You saved him, Kaelen. You chose him over catching Valerius. That matters."

"It won't matter if Valerius destroys the city," Kaelen said quietly.

"Then we stop him." Elara stood, offering her hand. "Together. The way it was always meant to be."

Kaelen took her hand and rose, ignoring the protest from his battered body. He looked back one last time at Berenger's empty armor—a ghost of his past, finally laid to rest.

"One more fight," he said.

"One more," Elara agreed. "And then we're done. No more corrupt priests. No more impossible choices. Just... us."

Through the tether, he felt her certainty, her fierce love, her absolute refusal to let him face this alone.

They walked toward the exit together, hand in hand. Behind them, Berenger's empty armor lay silent in the moonlight, a monument to a man who had died for a lie because he couldn't bear to live with the truth.

Ahead of them, in the heart of the Cathedral, the High Priest was making his final stand.

The Great Hall stood empty now, a tomb for one false god.

But there was still one more to face.

And this time, they would face him together.

Chapter Twenty-Two

THE HIGH PRIEST'S FALL

The inner sanctum of the High Priest was a sanctuary built on stolen lives.

Kaelen and Elara descended through the Cathedral's heart, following a spiral staircase that wound deeper and deeper into the ancient foundations. The walls here were older than the Order itself—pre-dating the theocracy by centuries. These stones remembered when Oakhaven had been free.

The air grew colder with each step, and through the tether, they felt each other's determination hardening into something unbreakable.

"He'll be desperate," Elara said quietly, her neon-pink glow the only light in the darkness. "Wounded animals are the most dangerous."

"Good," Kaelen replied, his silver sword humming in his hand. "I'm tired of fighting careful enemies. Let him be desperate. Let him show us exactly who he is when the mask finally comes off."

They reached the bottom—a circular chamber carved from living rock. The walls were lined with shelves holding relics and texts, each one carefully preserved, each one a piece of the Order's carefully curated history. A massive crystalline dome overhead focused moonlight into a single, concentrated beam that illuminated a desk made of white marble and fossilized bone.

And standing before that desk, blood seeping through his white robes from the wounds he'd taken in the tower, was High Priest Valerius.

He wasn't alone.

Hovering in the center of the room, suspended in a web of silver chains that radiated from the walls like a spider's web, was the Founders' Mirror. It was enormous—easily ten feet across—and its surface rippled with an oily, wrong sheen that made Elara's magic recoil instinctively.

This wasn't just a mirror. It was a wound. A crack in reality that the first Order priests had torn open and then learned to weaponize.

Valerius's hands rested on a control pedestal carved with runes that glowed a sickly white. His face was gaunt, aged decades in the hours since the tower confrontation. The stolen life-force that had sustained him was failing, burning out like a candle guttering in its final moments.

But his eyes—those were still sharp. Still calculating. Still absolutely convinced of his own righteousness.

"Kaelen," Valerius said, not bothering to turn around. His voice was the same cold, measured tone Kaelen remembered from countless audiences. "I suppose Berenger failed to remind you of your vows. A pity. He was always reliable, if unimaginative."

"Berenger's dead," Kaelen said flatly, stepping into the room. Elara moved with him, their movements synchronized through years of fighting side-by-side and the deeper synchronization of the soul-tether. "He died loyal to you. To the lie you built. Does that bother you at all?"

Valerius finally turned. His face was less human than Kaelen remembered—skin pulled too tight over sharp bones, eyes sunk deep into sockets that seemed to hold nothing but cold void. He didn't look like a man anymore. He looked like something wearing a man's skin.

"Bother me?" Valerius repeated, a thin smile touching his bloodless lips. "Why would it? Berenger understood his purpose. He was a tool—a well-crafted one, certainly, but a tool nonetheless. Tools break. It's the nature of matter to decay."

"Is that what we all were to you?" Elara asked, her voice sharp as broken glass. "Tools? The paladins, the Purifiers, your own son—just instruments for your 'perfect vision'?"

"Of course," Valerius said, as if the answer was obvious. "The world requires order. And people—people are fundamentally chaotic. They question. They doubt. They resist. Left to their own devices, they descend into anarchy and suffering. Someone has to guide them. Someone has to make the hard choices they're too weak to make themselves."

He walked to the center of the room, closer to the Founders' Mirror. His white robes rustled, and Kaelen could see the full extent of his wounds now—deep gashes across his torso where Vane's blade had struck, burns on his palms from grabbing the Prime Lens, and something worse: a spreading network of black veins that looked disturbingly like the void-corruption they'd seen in the Hollowed.

Valerius was dying. And he was taking the city with him.

"The void-rifts were brilliant, if I may say so myself," the High Priest continued, almost conversational. "A controlled threat. Just dangerous enough to keep the populace grateful for our protection, just manageable enough that we could 'save' them whenever necessary. It was a perfect ecosystem."

"It was mass murder," Kaelen said, his voice dropping to something cold and dangerous. "You killed thousands to maintain power."

"I killed thousands to save millions," Valerius corrected. "Without the Order's guidance, this entire region would have collapsed into warlordism and barbarism. The proto-Order understood this. They created the first void-rift as a demonstration of divine authority. I simply... refined the technique."

His hands moved across the control pedestal, and the Founders' Mirror began to hum. The sound was wrong—too low, felt more than heard, vibrating in the bones and teeth.

"This mirror," Valerius said, his voice taking on an almost reverent tone, "is the key. The first successful weaponization of Holy Light. My predecessors discovered that if you focus divine energy through a flawed lens—one with intentional imperfections—it doesn't purify. It corrupts. It tears reality apart and creates... absence. Void. Shadow. The very thing we were supposed to fight."

The mirror's surface began to swirl, colors that shouldn't exist bleeding across its surface. Through the tether, Kaelen felt Elara's growing horror as she recognized what was happening.

"You're creating a rift," she breathed. "Here. Now. In the heart of the city."

"Not just any rift," Valerius said, his smile widening. "The ultimate rift. Powered by three centuries of stolen life-force, channeled through the original lens, anchored to the very foundations of Oakhaven. When it opens, it will consume everything within ten miles. The city. The Cathedral. Every witness to my supposed 'failure.'"

"And you with it," Kaelen pointed out.

"A necessary sacrifice," Valerius said calmly. "If I cannot rule, then let there be nothing left to rule. Let the void consume it all, and in a generation, the Order will rebuild. They'll tell stories of the heroic High Priest who died trying to stop the great darkness. They'll make me a martyr. And the cycle will begin again."

His hands pressed down on the final activation rune.

The Founders' Mirror screamed.

*   *   *

The rift that began to form wasn't like the others Kaelen and Elara had seen.

This was primordial. Original. The source.

The center of the mirror didn't just turn black—it became the absence of everything. Not void as in emptiness, but void as in the active negation of existence. Looking at it was like staring at the moment before creation, the cosmic null-space that existed before the first light decided to exist.

But worse than the darkness was what happened at its edges.

The rift didn't have clean boundaries. It had fractal perimeters that grew and subdivided and grew again, each iteration creating new fingers of non-existence that reached out into reality like a cancer spreading through healthy tissue.

Where the fractal edges touched the air, reality didn't just break— it screamed. Elara could hear it through her death-attuned senses: the sound of the world being unmade, of the fundamental laws that held atoms together deciding they no longer applied.

The space around the rift began to warp. Not bending like gravity—this was dimensional folding. The chamber's walls appeared to exist in multiple places simultaneously, overlapping and intersecting in ways that made the eye rebel and the mind reject what it was seeing.

Colors bled out of existence in a spreading radius around the mirror. First went the reds, leached away into grey. Then oranges, yellows, greens—each wavelength of light systematically erased from the spectrum until only a sickly, bruised purple remained. And that too was fading, reality's palette being reduced to monochrome and then to something beyond even black and white.

Objects near the rift's influence began to flicker between states. A candelabra on Valerius's desk existed, then didn't exist, then existed again in a slightly different position, its reality uncertain, its existence negotiable. The very concept of "solid matter" was becoming optional in the rift's presence.

And through it all, there was movement that wasn't movement. The rift pulsed with a horrible, organic rhythm—expanding and contracting like a living heart, but each pulse pulled more reality into its maw. Each beat unmade a little more of the world.

Elara could see the microscopic level now, her necromancer's sight allowing her to perceive the dissolution happening at the smallest scale. Individual molecules of air near the rift weren't just breaking apart—they were forgetting how to be molecules. The bonds between atoms loosened, questioning their own existence, and then simply… stopped.

This was Void-Rift Stage 4. Not creation or growth or stabilization.

This was consumption. Reality ending. The universe digesting itself.

And it was spreading.

"Kaelen!" Elara screamed over the sound of the world coming apart. "We have to stop the mirror! If that rift stabilizes—"

"I know!" Kaelen was already moving, his sword raised, charging toward Valerius and the control pedestal.

The High Priest's hands moved in a practiced gesture, and from the walls, beams of concentrated Light erupted—not to create rifts this time, but to defend. Kaelen barely dodged the first beam, feeling the heat of it singe his hair. The second caught his shoulder, and he roared in pain as holy fire bit into his flesh.

"You cannot stop this!" Valerius shouted, his voice taking on a manic edge. "The ritual has begun! In three minutes, the rift will reach critical mass! In five, it will consume the Cathedral! In ten, all of Oakhaven will be erased!"

Kaelen tried to press forward, but the barrage of Light was relentless. Each beam forced him back, each near-miss reminded him of the Sun-Fire spear that had nearly killed him weeks ago.

He was going to die here. They both were. Unless—

"Elara!" he called through the tether, not with words but with pure intention. *Together. Like we practiced. Like we did against the Solar Flare.*

Through the bond, he felt her understanding, her fierce agreement, her absolute trust.

Elara's eyes blazed neon-pink, then shifted to that deep, dangerous violet that meant she was reaching for her darkest power. She didn't try to fight the Light. She did something else.

She grabbed the soul-tether.

The silver thread between them didn't just glow—it became a conduit. Elara poured her necromantic power through it, and Kaelen opened himself to receive it. Death magic flooded into him, mixing with the residual Light he still carried from his paladin training.

The combination should have been impossible. Light and Shadow. Life and Death. Order and Chaos.

But through the tether—through their love, their trust, their absolute certainty in each other—it became something new.

Rose-gold energy erupted from Kaelen's body, neither pink nor white but a perfect fusion of both. He didn't block the next Light-beam. He absorbed it, pulled it through the tether to Elara, who transmuted it into raw power and sent it back.

They became a closed circuit. A perpetual engine of mutual protection and amplification.

"Impossible," Valerius breathed, his assault faltering as he stared at them in disbelief. "You can't—Light and Shadow cannot coexist! The fundamental laws—"

"Are just guidelines," Elara finished, her voice overlapping with Kaelen's through the tether. They spoke as one now, two voices in perfect harmony. "And we've never been very good at following rules."

Kaelen charged.

This time, when the Light-beams struck him, they didn't burn. They were absorbed, transmuted, and sent back at twice the intensity. He was a mirror himself now—not of glass and silver, but of love and absolute partnership.

His sword came down on the control pedestal.

Valerius moved with desperate speed, intercepting the blade with his bare hands. The High Priest's palms were already scarred from the Prime Lens, and now Kaelen's silver edge bit deep, cutting through flesh and bone.

But Valerius didn't flinch. Didn't scream. With inhuman strength born of centuries-old life-force and pure, fanatical conviction, he held the blade.

"You think killing me stops this?" Valerius hissed, his face inches from Kaelen's. His breath smelled of rot and incense. "I AM the ritual! My life-force powers the mirror! When I die, it all releases at once! The rift will consume everything instantly!"

"Then I guess you don't get to die yet," Kaelen said grimly.

He let go of his sword—left it embedded in Valerius's hands—and grabbed the High Priest by the throat.

"Elara! The mirror!"

She understood immediately. While Kaelen held Valerius, preventing him from completing the ritual or dying and triggering the catastrophic release, Elara turned her full attention to the Founders' Mirror.

She'd destroyed mirrors before. But never one like this. Never one that was actively generating a world-ending rift.

She reached out with her necromancy, searching for a purchase point, a way in. The mirror was ancient, but it was still made of matter. And all matter eventually died.

She found it—microscopic fractures in the silver surface, tiny flaws that had accumulated over three centuries of use. Entropy. Decay. The natural breakdown that came for everything eventually.

Elara spoke to those cracks. Whispered to them in the language of endings. Encouraged them to do what they'd always wanted to do: spread. Grow. Finish the job.

The mirror didn't shatter. It aged.

Three hundred years of accumulated wear happened in three seconds. The silver surface tarnished, pitted, corroded. The crystal backing cracked, then spider-webbed, then turned to powder.

The chains holding it began to rust, metal oxidizing at impossible speeds.

And the rift—

The rift screamed as its anchor point dissolved. Without the mirror to stabilize it, to feed it, to give it purpose, the void began to collapse in on itself. Reality rushed back in to fill the space, nature abhorring the vacuum.

But there was still the life-force. Valerius's three centuries of stolen power, currently keeping the High Priest alive despite his wounds.

That energy had to go somewhere.

"Kaelen," Elara said quietly, and through the tether he felt her terrible realization. "We have to let him go. When the mirror breaks, the energy will backlash. If he's still alive when it happens..."

"Everyone dies," Kaelen finished. He looked down at Valerius, at the man who had orchestrated so much suffering, who had killed his own son with casual disregard, who was still trying to destroy the world out of spite.

He thought about Berenger's last words. Thank you for ending this.

Sometimes mercy was killing. And sometimes it was letting someone face the consequences of their own choices.

Kaelen released his grip.

Valerius staggered back, pulling Kaelen's sword from his hands with a wet, tearing sound. The High Priest looked at them—at the fallen paladin and the risen necromancer, at the impossible love that had defeated his perfect order—and for the first time, Kaelen saw something that might have been fear in those cold eyes.

"You've doomed us all," Valerius whispered.

"No," Elara said gently. "You did that. We're just making sure you can't take anyone else with you."

The Founders' Mirror gave one final, crystalline shriek and shattered.

The backlash was instantaneous.

All the life-force Valerius had stolen—centuries worth of stolen years, countless deaths compressed into a single instant—reversed. The energy didn't release outward. It imploded, drawn back to its source like a rubber band snapping back.

Valerius didn't have time to scream.

One moment he was standing there, sword in hand, facing his executioners.

The next, he was unmaking.

It started at his extremities. His fingers dissolved first, turning translucent, then transparent, then simply ceasing to be. The effect spread up his arms, across his chest, his face a rictus of silent horror as he felt himself being erased from existence.

Not killed. Not consumed. Unmade. Every cell, every atom, every particle that had made up the High Priest deciding simultaneously that it preferred not to exist.

The Light he'd worshipped his entire life was reclaiming its loan. And the interest was everything.

In five seconds, it was over.

High Priest Valerius ceased to exist. Not even ash remained. Just a pile of empty robes and a profound, ringing silence.

The rift was gone. The mirror was destroyed. The sanctum stood empty except for two exhausted people holding each other upright through sheer force of will.

Kaelen and Elara stood in the wreckage, their hands still clasped, the rose-gold light of their combined magic slowly fading back to silver.

"Is it over?" Elara asked, her voice small and tired.

Kaelen looked around the chamber—at the empty robes, at the destroyed mirror, at the relics that would need to be catalogued and judged, at the three-hundred-year-old lie that had finally, irrevocably, been exposed.

"The fighting's over," he said quietly, pulling her close. "But the work... the work is just beginning."

Through the destroyed dome overhead, they could hear it—the sound of thousands of people in the streets above. Not screaming. Not rioting.

Talking. Processing. Beginning to ask the questions the Order had spent centuries suppressing.

Elara leaned her head against his chest, listening to the steady beat of his heart. They were both battered, burned, exhausted beyond measure. But they were alive. Together.

"We did it," she whispered.

"We did," Kaelen agreed, pressing a kiss to the top of her head. "You were magnificent."

"We were magnificent," she corrected. "Together. Always together."

The rose-gold light pulsed one more time between them—not magic now, just love. Pure, unconditional, unshakable.

They'd torn down a theocracy. Exposed a centuries-old lie. Saved a city.

And they'd done it together.

"Come on," Elara said finally, tugging him toward the stairs. "Let's go see what kind of world we accidentally created."

They walked out of the inner sanctum hand in hand, two figures silhouetted against the dawn light streaming through the broken dome above, leaving behind the empty robes of a dead god and stepping into a future that was terrifying, uncertain, and finally, finally free.

Chapter Twenty-Three

THE NEW DAWN

One month after the fall of the High Priest, Oakhaven looked different.

Not in the dramatic way—the Cathedral still dominated the skyline, its white spires reaching toward a sky that seemed bluer now, cleaner, as if the air itself had been holding its breath and could finally exhale. The buildings were the same, the streets followed the same ancient paths.

But the people had changed. And that made all the difference.

The morning air in Oakhaven didn't taste of incense and ash anymore. It tasted of damp earth from the morning rain, of bread baking in the ovens of the market square, and of peonies—so many peonies, planted in window boxes and garden plots across the city in a silent, organic memorial to the dead who had finally been allowed to rest.

Elara stood on the balcony of the newly established Protectorate headquarters—a building that had once housed the Order's administrative offices but now served as the seat of the provisional council government. She leaned against the stone railing, her neon-pink hair catching the morning light, and watched the city wake up.

In the Cathedral Square below, the massive pyre where the Order had planned to burn her and Kaelen had been dismantled. In its place, builders were constructing something new—a memorial garden, designed by a committee of citizens who'd voted on every detail. At its center would stand a fountain carved with the names of everyone who'd died in the void-rifts, both the real victims and those the Order had falsely claimed as casualties.

The execution square was gone. In its place: a market. Honest trade instead of holy terror.

"You're brooding again," Kaelen's voice came from the doorway, warm with affection and gentle teasing.

Elara didn't turn, but she smiled. Through the silver tether—still present at their wrists, though it had transformed into something that felt less like a chain and more like a choice—she felt his approach. Felt the steady warmth of his presence, the bone-deep contentment that came from a man who had finally stopped running from himself.

"I'm not brooding," she protested. "I'm observing. Thoughtfully. There's a difference."

"You're thinking about the people we couldn't save." Kaelen stepped onto the balcony and wrapped his arms around her from behind, his chin resting on top of her head. Without the golden armor—which had been melted down and recast into bells for the new memorial garden—he moved more freely, more comfortably in his own skin. "I can feel it through the bond."

"Damn tether," Elara muttered, but she leaned back into his warmth. "Yes, I'm thinking about them. The villages that were erased before we could stop it. The people who died believing the Order's lies. The ones we were too late to help."

"We cannot save everyone," Kaelen said quietly, his arms tightening around her. "I've learned that the hard way. But we saved the ones we could. We gave them the truth. That has to be enough."

Below them, a translucent figure drifted through the market—one of the Ancestors who had chosen to remain visible, integrated into the daily life of the city. A baker waved at the ghost, asking for advice on a recipe that had been passed down through generations. The spirit smiled and began gesturing, explaining something about the proper ratio of flour to water.

It had taken weeks for the living to adjust to the constant presence of the dead. There had been fear at first, revulsion from those who'd been taught that spirits were corruptions to be destroyed. But slowly—so slowly—people had begun to remember. To recognize grandmothers and great-uncles, to hear stories about their own childhoods told by people who'd watched them grow.

The dead weren't monsters. They were memory made manifest. And Oakhaven was learning to listen.

"The Council wants to make an official announcement today," Kaelen said, his voice shifting to the professional tone he used when discussing policy. "About the Final Rite."

"Necromancy legalized," Elara said, testing the words. Even after a month, they still felt strange. "I'm going to need a proper office. And a secretary who doesn't faint when I summon spirits for consultations. And possibly business cards. Do necromancers have business cards?"

"You're the first legal one in three hundred years. You can set the precedent."

Elara turned in his arms, looking up at the man who'd become her partner in every sense of the word. Kaelen had been officially appointed to the Protectorate Council as Military Advisor—a position he'd accepted with reluctance but was performing with the same dedication he'd once given to the Order. But now, that dedication was tempered with wisdom, with the understanding that duty without compassion was just tyranny with better marketing.

"Have you heard from Jaxon?" Elara asked.

Kaelen's expression softened. "A letter arrived yesterday. He's recovering well—the Light-burns are healed, and he's working with the Unchained to establish proper communication networks across the territories. He says the resistance is transforming into something more like… a civic organization. Helping rebuild what the Order destroyed."

"Smart boy," Elara said approvingly. "He turned his pain into purpose."

"He learned from the best," Kaelen said, then paused. "He also asked about you. Wanted to know if the 'lady with the pink streaks in her hair who saved both our lives' was doing well."

"I'm doing magnificently," Elara said with exaggerated grandeur. "I've been pardoned, legalized, and given an official government position as 'Consultant for Ancestral Relations.' I have power, prestige, and a very attractive former paladin who brings me tea in the mornings without being asked. Life is excellent."

"I brought you tea once," Kaelen protested. "And you complained it was too hot."

"It was too hot. I have a refined palate."

Through the tether, she felt his amusement, his love, his absolute contentment with this—with her, with the life they were building in the ruins of the Order's theocracy.

A polite cough from the doorway interrupted their moment. General Vane's spectral form materialized, his azure eyes glowing with their usual intensity. The ancient ghost had become a fixture in the Protectorate headquarters, serving as an unofficial historian and advisor on military matters.

"Apologies for the interruption," Vane's gravelly voice rumbled, "but the Council is gathering for the morning session. They'll want to finalize the Memorial Day proclamation, and there's the matter of what to do with the remaining Cathedral infrastructure."

"The mirrors are all destroyed?" Elara asked.

"Every last one," Vane confirmed. "Melted down and repurposed. Some of the silver went into the memorial fountain. The rest was distributed to artisans across the city with explicit instructions that it never be used for 'holy purposes' again. Just art. Just beauty."

"Good," Kaelen said. "And the Catacombs?"

"Open to the public as of three days ago. People are visiting their ancestors, leaving flowers, telling stories. It's..." Vane paused, and for a moment his ancient, war-hardened demeanor cracked. "It's what we fought for. Three hundred years ago, and again last month. The right to be remembered."

Elara felt tears prick at her eyes. She'd spent so much of her life being told that her work was foul, that giving voice to the dead was corruption. To see it recognized as holy—truly holy, not the manufactured righteousness of the Order—felt like vindication she hadn't known she needed.

"Arthur's been helping with the tours," Vane added, his tone shifting to something that might have been amusement if ghosts could be amused. "He's apparently quite popular with the visitors. Very enthusiastic about explaining proper tomb etiquette and the historical significance of various burial practices."

"Of course he is," Elara laughed, wiping her eyes. "He's been waiting two hundred years for someone to appreciate his expertise on the 1422 Tax Reform. Now he has a captive audience."

"Literally captive," Vane agreed. "He corners them in the Founders' Vault and won't let them leave until they've heard the full lecture series."

"I should probably talk to him about that."

"Please do. We're getting complaints."

The ghost general faded back into transparency, returning to whatever spectral duties occupied his time, and Kaelen and Elara were alone again on the balcony.

"We did it," Elara said quietly, looking out over the city. "We actually did it. We tore down a three-hundred-year-old theocracy, exposed their lies, and didn't die in the process. That has to be some kind of record."

"We had help," Kaelen reminded her. "Vane. The Ancestors. Every person who chose to believe the truth instead of the comfortable lie."

"Still. We're alive. Together. That's more than I expected when you arrested me in that graveyard." She turned to face him fully, her hands coming up to rest on his chest. The handprint scar she'd left when she'd pulled the Sun-Fire out of him was visible through his open shirt collar—a permanent reminder of the death she'd cheated, the love that had saved them both.

"The Council session," Kaelen said reluctantly. "We should go."

"We should," Elara agreed, not moving.

"They're waiting for us."

"They can wait five more minutes."

Kaelen smiled—the real smile, the one that crinkled the corners of his eyes and made him look years younger than the weight he carried. He leaned down and kissed her, soft and unhurried, the kind of kiss that spoke of having all the time in the world because they'd fought for the right to have a future.

When they finally pulled apart, the sun had fully risen over Oakhaven, gilding the white spires of the Cathedral in honest gold instead of the artificial glare of the Order's mirrors.

It was a new dawn.

And for the first time in three hundred years, it felt like hope.

. . .

Inside the private chambers of the Sanctum—the section of the Cathedral complex that had been converted into living quarters for the Protectorate's leadership—the "Happily Ever After" was quieter and far more honest than any fairy tale.

The room was smaller than Elara had expected when they'd first been offered permanent residence in the city. After months on the road, sleeping in caves and dangerous inns and one memorable night in a barn where Cinder had eaten her favorite scarf, she'd imagined something grand. Something with dramatic curtains and possibly a chandelier.

Instead, they'd chosen a modest suite on the third floor—large enough to be comfortable, small enough to feel like home. The windows looked out over the memorial garden, and at night they could hear the fountain running, a constant gentle reminder of the names carved into its stone.

Elara sat on the edge of the bed, kicking off her boots with a sigh of relief that was probably inappropriate for someone who was supposed to be a dignified government official. The Council session had run long—debates about land redistribution, arguments about how to handle former Order members who claimed they "didn't know" about the corruption, discussions about establishing diplomatic relations with neighboring territories who were suddenly very interested in how Oakhaven had managed to overthrow a theocracy without collapsing into chaos.

It was exhausting. Important, necessary, vital work.

But exhausting.

Kaelen was at the washbasin, his shirt already discarded, his scarred back visible in the candlelight. The handprint on his ribs glowed faintly pink in the dim room—a permanent reminder of Elara's magic, of the moment she'd chosen to save him instead of saving herself.

"The tether is changing," Kaelen said quietly, staring at the silver thread that connected his wrist to hers. It was barely visible now— more a shimmer than a solid line, like spider silk catching the light.

"Changing how?" Elara asked, though she'd felt it too. The bond between them had evolved over the months. What had started as a prison, a forced connection designed to keep her contained, had transformed into something else entirely.

"It's loosening," Kaelen said, his voice carefully neutral. "The mages say the soul-anchor is stable enough now that we could sever it. Cleanly. Without the... explosive death complications."

Elara's heart did something complicated in her chest. "Is that what you want? To be free of me?"

Kaelen turned, crossing the room in three quick strides. He knelt in front of her, his hands taking hers, his eyes intense in the candlelight.

"I don't want to be free of you," he said, his voice rough with emotion. "I want to choose you. Not because a ritual bound us together, not because we're trapped by magical necessity, but because I love you. Because you're the best thing that's ever happened to me, even though you ruined my life, destroyed my career, and got me branded a traitor by the only family I'd ever known."

"When you put it that way, I sound very inconvenient," Elara said, but her voice was thick with tears.

"You are inconvenient," Kaelen agreed, a smile tugging at his lips. "You're also brilliant, compassionate, sarcastic to the point of being a social hazard, and the only person I've ever met who makes me want to be better than the man the Order built."

He reached up, cupping her face in his hands, his thumbs brushing away the tears that had started to fall.

"So no," he said softly. "I don't want to sever the tether. But I want it to be a choice. For both of us. Not a curse. Not a chain. A promise."

Elara leaned into his touch, her heart so full it felt like it might burst. "You're very romantic for a man who spent a decade arresting people for minor legal infractions."

"I've had a good teacher," Kaelen replied. "She's taught me that sometimes breaking the rules is the holiest thing you can do."

They stayed like that for a long moment—forehead to forehead, breathing the same air, the silver tether pulsing with warmth between them.

"I choose you too," Elara whispered. "Every day. Every moment. For as long as we both shall live."

"And possibly after," Kaelen added with a small smile. "Given your professional expertise in the afterlife."

"Definitely after," Elara confirmed. "I'm not letting you escape me that easily."

He kissed her then—deep and slow and full of promise. When he pulled back, his expression had shifted to something more serious.

"There's something else," he said. "The Council wants to formalize our... partnership. Officially. They're calling it a 'civic union' since marriage has too many Order connotations, but—"

"Are you asking me to marry you?" Elara interrupted, her eyes wide.

"I'm asking if you want to make this permanent," Kaelen said carefully. "In the eyes of the law. Not just the soul-bond. A choice we make publicly, together."

Elara stared at him, this man who had arrested her seventeen times, who had chased her across the borderlands, who had thrown away everything to stand beside her in the ruins of his former life.

"Yes," she said simply. "A thousand times yes."

The smile that broke across Kaelen's face was radiant. He pulled her close, kissing her again, deeper this time, with the kind of passion that came from knowing there was no longer any reason to hold back.

They fell back onto the bed together, a tangle of limbs and whispered promises and the silver tether glowing rose-gold between them. The Council could wait. The world could wait.

Tonight was theirs alone.

And as the moon rose over Oakhaven, casting silver light through the windows, two people who had torn down an empire found something far more precious in each other's arms.

Not just love.

Not just partnership.

But home.

Chapter Twenty-Four

THE SILVER THREAD

Inside the private chambers of the Sanctum, three weeks after the proposal, the peace they'd fought for finally felt real.

The room was quiet except for the gentle sound of rain against the windows. Elara lay curled against Kaelen's side, her head on his chest, listening to the steady rhythm of his heartbeat. His hand traced lazy patterns on her shoulder, and through the tether she could feel his contentment, his peace, his bone-deep happiness.

This was what they'd fought for. Not grand pronouncements or political victories, but moments like this. Simple. Quiet. Together.

"The Council approved the memorial design," Kaelen said softly, his voice rumbling in his chest. "Construction starts next week. They're using the melted-down armor from the Purifiers who surrendered. Turning weapons into art."

"Poetic," Elara murmured, her fingers tracing the rose-gold handprint scar on his ribs. "Berenger would have hated it."

"Good." There was no bitterness in his voice anymore, just acceptance. "He spent his whole life believing symbols mattered more than people. Let his legacy be a reminder to choose differently."

Elara tilted her head up to look at him. In the candlelight, without his armor, without the weight of the Order's expectations, Kaelen looked younger. Softer. Happy.

"I love you," she said simply. Not dramatic or flowery—just truth.

"I know," he replied, a smile tugging at his lips. "The soul-bond makes it hard to hide."

"That's not what I mean." She sat up slightly, propping herself on one elbow so she could see his face properly. "I mean I choose to love you. Every day. Bond or no bond. Tether or no tether. You could sever it tomorrow and I'd still be here."

Kaelen's hand came up to cup her face, his thumb brushing across her cheekbone. "I'm not severing it. Ever. This—" he gestured to the silver thread between their wrists, barely visible now, more suggestion than substance, "—this is the best thing that ever happened to me. Even if it started as a prison."

"Especially because it started as a prison," Elara corrected. "It forced us to actually see each other. No running. No hiding. Just… truth."

He pulled her down for a kiss, slow and deep and full of promise. When they broke apart, Elara settled back against his chest, and for a long moment, they simply existed together in comfortable silence.

Then the tether went cold.

Not the comfortable warmth they'd grown used to. Not even the neutral temperature of rest. This was ice. Absolute, bone-deep cold that made Elara gasp and Kaelen jolt upright.

The silver thread between their wrists didn't just cool—it turned black. Void-black. The same terrifying absence they'd seen in the rifts.

"Kaelen—" Elara started, but her voice died as she stared at their joined wrists.

The tether was writhing. Pulsing. Warning.

A sharp tap at the window made them both jump.

Through the rain-streaked glass, Elara could see a bird perched on the sill. But this was no ordinary raven. Its feathers were matted with frost—actual ice crystals that glittered in the candlelight, impossible in the mild autumn weather. Its eyes weren't black. They were burning with a spectral azure light, but colder than Vane's ghostly gaze. Ancient. Wrong.

The bird tapped again, more insistently, then dropped something onto the stone sill before taking flight into the storm.

Kaelen approached the window slowly, his hand instinctively reaching for a sword that wasn't there. He picked up the object with careful fingers.

It was a coin. Iron, so cold it burned his skin where it touched. On its face was a symbol neither of them recognized—a crown made of jagged ice, rendered in such exquisite detail that each individual barb seemed to shimmer with frost.

The moment Kaelen's skin made contact, the vision hit them both through the tether.

They saw the far North—a region beyond even the Grey Wastes, a land of permafrost and endless winter that existed at the edge of the known world. They saw a wall of ice that had stood for millennia, taller than mountains, stretching from horizon to horizon. A barrier. A prison.

Keeping something contained.

Keeping something locked away.

And they saw that wall shattering.

Not slowly. Not with warning. The ice exploded outward in massive chunks, each piece the size of a Cathedral, calving away and crashing into frozen seas with the sound of the world ending. Through the breach, something was emerging from the permafrost.

A throne.

It rose from the ice like a tooth being pulled from a frozen jaw—massive, ancient, carved from the bones of creatures that had died before humans learned to make fire. The bones weren't clean white. They were stained with something dark, something that pulsed with a horrible organic rhythm.

And sitting on that throne, crowned in jagged ice that grew directly from his skull, was a figure.

He was impossibly tall—taller than Vane, taller than any human had a right to be. His skin was the blue-white of frostbite, stretched too tight over bones that jutted at wrong angles. His eyes were empty sockets, but in those voids burned a light that was somehow darker than darkness—a negative radiance that consumed rather than illuminated.

He wore robes made of frozen souls. Elara could see them—translucent forms trapped in the ice that draped his skeletal frame, their mouths open in eternal screams that no one could hear.

In his hand, he held a staff carved from a single massive icicle. At its top was mounted a human skull, but this skull was wrong. Too many eye sockets. Too many teeth. As if multiple heads had been fused together into something that should never have existed.

The figure stood, and the sound of ice cracking echoed through the vision like the world's spine breaking.

When he spoke, his voice didn't come from his mouth. It came from everywhere—from the ice, from the frozen ground, from the very air itself. And it spoke directly into their minds through the blackened tether:

"The Sun has set. The Order has fallen. The Light that bound me weakens."

The figure turned his empty gaze directly toward them—toward Kaelen and Elara, hundreds of miles away, seeing them through space and time and the thin barrier between the living and the dead.

"The necromancer thinks she's won. The fallen paladin believes he's free. But you do not understand the price of your victory."

The staff struck the ground, and across the vision, the ice wall shattered completely. Behind the King, an army was revealed—not soldiers, but corpses. Thousands of them. Hundreds of thousands. The accumulated dead of millennia, all bound to his will, all moving with that same horrible, synchronized precision.

"The High Priest stole life to sustain his pathetic empire. But that life-force belonged to me. Every soul he 'consumed'—he borrowed. Every year he lived beyond his allotted time—stolen from my domain. And now, the debt is due."

The King's skeletal hand reached out, pointing directly at Elara through the vision. She felt it—a cold so profound it burned, a claim being staked on her very existence.

"You, necromancer, hold the keys to death's gate. You command what should be mine. You have taken liberties with powers you do not comprehend."

Then his gaze shifted to Kaelen, and the cold became absolute.

"And you, paladin of the dead Light. You carry the stolen fire in your veins still. Sun-touched. Soul-bound. You are the bridge between Light and Shadow that should not exist."

The King leaned forward on his throne, his voice dropping to something almost intimate, almost amused:

"You destroyed the Order to save your pathetic little city. Noble. Touching. But you broke the seals, children. The High Priest's mirrors weren't just weapons—they were chains. Binding me. Keeping me locked beyond the Wall. And you shattered every. Last. One."

The vision pulsed with dark satisfaction.

"The King of Hollows comes to reclaim his stolen kingdom. The debt will be paid in full. In flesh. In souls. In the screaming, frozen eternity you've earned with your meddling."

The figure raised his staff, and across the frozen wasteland, his army began to march. Not walking—sliding across the ice with impossible speed, their frozen corpses gliding like skaters, covering miles in seconds.

"I will arrive with winter's first breath. Three months. Perhaps four, if the snows are merciful. And when I reach your warm, living city, when my army stands at your gates, you will understand the truth:"

The King's voice became a whisper that echoed like thunder:

"The Sun was never your enemy. It was your shield. And you have extinguished it."

The vision shattered like glass.

Kaelen and Elara were back in their room, gasping for air, clutching each other. The coin in Kaelen's hand was so cold it had frozen to his palm, leaving a burn in the exact shape of the ice-crown when he finally pried it free.

For a long moment, neither of them could speak.

Then Elara laughed. A single, slightly hysterical sound that became a groan.

"We just saved the world," she said weakly. "We're supposed to get at least a year off before the next apocalypse."

"Apparently the universe doesn't believe in vacation time," Kaelen replied, his voice tight with shock.

He looked at the coin, still smoking with cold on the bedside table. Looked at the blackened tether that was slowly, reluctantly, fading back to silver. Looked at Elara—the woman he'd just promised to spend his life with, who was now being claimed by some ancient dead king from beyond the world's edge.

"We need help," he said quietly. "More than Vane and the Ancestors can provide. If that thing is really coming—if it has an army of the frozen dead—"

"We need a bigger army," Elara finished, echoing her words from so many months ago. "One that can fight ice with fire. Death with life. Void with—"

She stopped, her eyes going wide with sudden, terrible understanding.

"The tether," she breathed. "That's why it turned black. That's why it reacted. Kaelen, the King didn't just send us a warning. He sent us a message. He's telling us that our bond—the soul-anchor we created—it's the key."

"The key to what?"

"To fighting him." Elara grabbed his hands, her neon-pink eyes blazing with the fierce, manic energy that always emerged when she was working through an impossible problem. "Think about it. The High Priest used mirrors to focus Light into Void. But we did the opposite—we used the tether to blend Light and Shadow into something new. Rose-gold. Neither pure Light nor pure Death, but both. Together."

Kaelen's mind was already racing ahead, seeing the connections. "The King said I carry stolen fire. The Sun-touched power I got from the Order. And you have command over death. If we could amplify it—use the tether not just between us, but to anchor more people, more power—"

"We'd need others like us," Elara said. "Pairs. Bonds. People who can bridge the gap between Light and Shadow without being consumed by either."

"Where do we find them?"

Elara's smile was sharp and bright and absolutely feral. "We make them. We teach them. We build an army of the soul-bound who can fight death itself."

She pulled him close, her forehead pressed against his, the tether between them pulsing with renewed warmth—silver shot through with threads of rose-gold.

"The King of Hollows thinks we're isolated. That we destroyed our only defenses. That we're weak."

"But we're not," Kaelen said, understanding dawning. "Because we didn't just tear down the Order. We showed people there was another way. And they're listening."

"The Unchained," Elara said. "Jaxon's network. The Ancestors who chose to stay. Every person who stood in that square and saw the truth. They're not just witnesses anymore. They're potential."

Through the window, the storm was intensifying. Thunder rolled across the sky, and in the distance, Kaelen could have sworn he heard the sound of ice cracking.

Three months. Maybe four.

They had until winter.

"We're going to need to call in every favor we have," Kaelen said. "Reach out to the territories beyond Oakhaven. Find every mage, every warrior, every person with even a spark of power who's willing to learn."

"We're going to need to visit places even I find creepy," Elara added. "Old graves. Ancient battlefields. Anywhere the boundary between life and death is thin. If the King has an army of the frozen dead, we'll need an army of the righteous dead."

"General Vane isn't going to like this."

"General Vane is going to love this," Elara corrected. "He's been waiting three hundred years for a real war. One where the enemy isn't his own corrupted brothers."

Kaelen pulled her into his arms, holding her tight, breathing in the scent of peonies and graveyard dirt and life. Through the tether, he felt her fear—she was terrified, genuinely terrified, in a way she hadn't been even when facing Valerius.

But he also felt her determination. Her absolute refusal to let some ancient dead king take away the future they'd just won.

"We'll stop him," Kaelen said quietly. "Just like we stopped the Order. Together."

"Together," Elara agreed. Then she pulled back, looking up at him with eyes that gleamed with mischief despite the fear. "But first, we're going to finish our interrupted evening. Because if the world's ending in three months, I am not spending tonight planning war councils."

"Elara—"

"Tomorrow," she said firmly, pulling him back toward the bed. "We'll save the world tomorrow. Tonight, we're just two people who love each other and refuse to let ancient evil ruin our romance."

Kaelen laughed despite everything—despite the vision, despite the threat, despite the knowledge that an army of frozen dead was currently marching toward everything they'd built.

Because she was right. They'd fought so hard for this—for the right to choose each other, to have moments of peace, to be something more than soldiers in someone else's war.

The King of Hollows could wait until morning.

They fell back into bed together, and as the storm raged outside, they found warmth in each other's arms. The tether glowed rose-gold between them—not a chain anymore, not a curse, but a promise.

A promise that whatever came next, they would face it together.

The Sun had set. The Order had fallen.

But the Golden Lion had found something worth fighting for that was stronger than any corrupted Light.

And the Necromancer had discovered that death was not the end—just the beginning of a new story.

*   *   *

Far to the north, beyond the Grey Wastes, beyond the permafrost, beyond the shattered ice wall, the King of Hollows settled back onto his throne of bone.

In his skeletal hand, he held a mirror—not of silver, but of ice so ancient and so cold it could freeze souls.

And in that mirror, he watched them. Watched the necromancer and her fallen paladin, wrapped in each other's arms, glowing with their pathetic mortal love.

"Enjoy your warmth, little sparks," he whispered to the frozen air. "Savor your victory. Because winter is coming. And I am patient."

His army of the frozen dead continued their march south, silent and inexorable as glaciers.

The debt would be paid.

And the King of Hollows always collected what he was owed.

THE SOUL-TETHER SAGA WILL CONTINUE IN

BOOK TWO: THE KING OF HOLLOWS

Coming Soon

About the author

ALIX ALORA writes dark romantasy for readers who believe that the best love stories are forged in fire, tempered by impossible choices, and proven through sacrifice. Alix's debut novel, The Necromancer & the Golden Knight, introduces readers to a world where necromancy is an act of mercy, paladins question their Gods, and the line between hero and villain depends entirely on who's writing the history books.

When not crafting morally grey characters and enemies-to-lovers tension that could power a small city, Alix can be found thinking about the future intersecting with the past, hosting or playing Dungeons & Dragons, marvelous bookstores, and arguing with fictional characters and AI models about their questionable opinions and life choices. Alix believes that mafic systems should have consequences, romances should be earned through emotional devastation, and every villain is just a protagonist whose story you haven't heard yet.

Alix is very private (which explains a lot about the necromancy), resides in a city that may or may not have its own haunted cathedral, and drink an irresponsible amount of water while debating whether these characters deserve happy endings or just deserve each other.

THE SOUL-TETHER SAGA

Book 1: The Necromancer & the Golden Knight

Books 2: The King of Hollows (coming 2026)

Book 3: [TBD] (coming 2026)

CONNECT WITH ALIX

Website: www.alixalora.com

Instagram: @alixalorabooks

TikTok: @alixalorabooks

Newsletter: alixalora.com/subscribe

For readers who like their romance dark,
their magic deadly, and their morals delightfully grey.

Thank you

www.ingramcontent.com/pod-product-compliance
Lightning Source LLC
Chambersburg PA
CBHW060413180626
46817CB00007B/2569